Martial Art
Essays from Beijing, 1760

Martial Art

Essays from

Beijing, 1760

by Michael A. DeMarco, MA

martial arts / fiction

"Contains the distillation of decades of careful study. Regardless of what tradition you study, you will find a great deal of wisdom in the pages of this book." —**Deborah Klens-Bigman, PhD,** Jun Shihan, Shinto Hatakage Ryu Iai Heijo

"What a masterpiece! Gem after gem after gem appear in these essays. This book is destined to sit alongside the *Tai Chi Classics* as a seminal guide of the arts." —**CJ Rhoads, DEd,** founder of Taijiquan Enthusiasts Organization

"A gem of a book . . . . Really a must read for all martial artists." —**Robert A. Servidio,** grandmaster, Liu Seong Royal Kuntao

"By following master Yang's clear and detailed instructions, all of us can definitely raise our level of skills." —**Dionisis Tsetselis,** head instructor, Hellenic Wu's Tai Chi Chuan Academy, Greece

"The reader is amazed how relevant these essays are to modern day martial arts." —**Abi Moriya,** head of martial arts discipline, Nat Holman School for Coaches and Instructors, Wingate Institute, Israel

"The essays provide revelations vital for understanding the ingenuity of Chinese martial arts." —**Zhu Shoutong, PhD,** director, Centre for Chinese History and Culture, University of Macau

"An ingenious framework for trying to insulate and reinforce the integrity of one's cross-cultural and technical understanding of Chinese martial arts." —**Philip H.J. Davies, PhD,** Deputy Director, Brunel University Centre for Intelligence & Security Studies; Kuntao Matjan

"Provides inspiration not just for martial artists, but also for dancers, actors, and athletes who will find many of the concepts of training and approaches to movement valuable." —**Kirstin Pauka, PhD,** director, Asian Theatre Program, University of Hawai'i at Mānoa

"DeMarco has presented to us the essence, not of Chinese martial arts, but of all martial arts. Sixty-four clear and precise chapters outline the essential knowledge a modern student should possess." —**Kim Taylor,** seventh dan iaido and sixth dan jodo

"For martial arts practitioners, the essays contain lessons from the fundamental to the intermediate to the profound. These essays can best be enjoyed one sip at a time, to savor their flavor and let the learnings slowly seep in."
—**Christopher Bates,** author, *The Wave Man*; master, American Bando; disciple of Hong Yi-Hsiang (洪懿祥)

"This story is brilliant. The book certainly allows one to better understand the connotations of the martial arts and Eastern culture. It is highly recommended." —**Xiong Naiqi** (熊迺祺), master, Xiong Yonghe martial arts system, Taiwan

"In addition to a succinct overview of the classical, philosophical foundations of the various Chinese martial traditions—that also influenced Japan—DeMarco provides physical examples and metaphorical explanations I can use when instructing my own students in analogous principles and techniques." —**Robert Wolfe,** fourth dan aikibudo; chief instructor, Itten Dojo, Mechanicsburg, PA

"Thoroughly enjoyable. The story is a wonderful vehicle for the explication of martial principles, drawing together threads of various aspects of life and culture to weave a tapestry of truth."
—**Russ Mason,** University of Delaware; instructor, Zheng Manqing lineage

"These essays are evenhanded, comprehensive, and timeless. This precious book is a gold mine of sober wisdom that will give the Chinese-style martial artist confirmation and confidence in the depth of their art. . . . important and thrilling to read."
—**Stephan Berwick,** founder, True Taiji; martial arts culturalist and advocate

Dedication

To the memories of these martial art teachers for sharing their knowledge and friendship: Arthur Sykes, Thomas Pepperman, Richard Lopez, Du Yuze and Yang Qingyu.

CONTENTS

Yang Mingbin's Essays

The themes in this book—drawn from Chinese history, culture, and martial arts experience—are entwined in a fictional narrative to animate events envisaged to have occurred during the mid-eighteenth century. From the outset, a thin veil separates fact from fiction. Our story starts with a discovery.

While conducting research at the Vatican Library on the Jesuit missions in China, two scholars find a folder of papers written in Chinese among documents belonging to Giuseppe Castiglione (1688–1766), a painter at the royal court in Beijing. The papers turn out to be written by a fellow court painter, Yang Mingbin (c. 1664–1765). Yang's handwritten essays provide revelations vital for understanding the ingenuity of Chinese martial arts.

Yang's text is organized under sixty-four subheadings. The author elucidates theory and practice methods in a fashion unlike any other writings on this subject. This is a rare, early text written during a transitional period for martial arts. It is the time when the Qing Dynasty (1644–1912) was at its peak of cultural splendor and expanding its borders by military expeditions. Cannons and smaller firearms show the Western influence, but traditional martial arts were ubiquitous at the village, province, and national levels.

Master Yang offers fascinating reading on all aspects of the Chinese fighting traditions. He places great emphasis on the importance of the "martial arts family" and the role of secrecy in lethal arts. The arts are also adapted for health and entertainment. All reflect an infusion of philosophy and practices from Buddhism, Daoism, and Confucianism. How one thinks affects how one practices martial arts.

Yang describes the qualities associated with different skill levels, from beginner to most advanced. As he does this, we learn secrets that set forth key ways for improving defensive and offensive applications. These topics include body alignment, coordination, spontaneity, naturalness, balance, distancing, relaxation, and power. The same principles apply to bare-hand and weapons practice, as well as martial arts for health. Yang's learning methodology for studying martial arts can be useful in other areas, as in his work as a master painter at court.

Background calligraphy from Giuseppe Castiglione's painting "One Hundred Horses," datable to 1723–25. Courtesy of the Metropolitan Museum of Art, New York City. CC0 1.0 Universal Public Domain Dedication. Self-portrait detail of Ren Xiong (1823–1857), Palace Museum, Beijing. Public domain.

Emperor Qianlong Inspecting Troops. Painting by Giuseppe Castiglione. Courtesy of The National Palace Museum, Taipei. Public domain.

It is exhilarating to write the foreword to this unique book, knowing it will become a treasured reading for any serious scholar or practitioner of martial arts. The following pages detail how fate led to the unexpected discovery of writings that sat hidden in plain sight for over two hundred years—the insightful notes made by Yang Mingbin, a martial arts master and royal court painter in Beijing. The significance of the handwritten pages is in the revelations provided for understanding Chinese martial arts of the eighteenth century. The author elucidates theory and practice methods in a fashion unlike any other writings on this subject. The chances were extremely slim in finding such important writings preserved in its leather folio. Learning about the discovery of the rare documents adds to our appreciation of the content itself.

Over the centuries, the Chinese have been strongly possessive of their highly effective combat traditions. Other cultures hold the same attitude. Why? It is only logical to be so when the arts are learned for their original lethal purpose. We now generally perceive the martial arts being studied as a performance art or mode of exercise—devoid of any profound knowledge of actual fighting applications. For some who do pursue the arts for combat purposes, the traditional precautions and ethical guidelines are often missing, and violent results unfortunately occur, a number certainly criminal.

Today discipleship ceremonies are rare. The need for blood oaths and poetic teaching ciphers is obsolete. Instruction is no longer behind closed doors, but open doors welcome thousands of students. Pay the fees and study your chosen art. Martial arts can be studied for a variety of reasons. A martial art can be seen as a form of exercise, a theatrical skill, a sport, or a system of self-defense. The wide spectrum of what the martial arts represent is not easy to comprehend.

Driven by the desire to understand the full significance of

martial traditions as they evolved over the centuries, serious practitioners and scholars learn from the leading representatives of styles and research written records. Since martial art knowledge was discreetly passed on primarily through oral transmission, the rare books and handwritten family documents are precious.

Of course, Chinese dynastic histories mention martial arts and their importance to the political and military establishments. There are references in poetry, gazetteers, and literature, including religious and medical documents. But any substantial book that focused solely on martial arts was rare prior to the late twentieth century. An outstanding military training manual and one of the earliest existing texts dealing with Chinese martial arts is the *New Book on Effective Military Techniques*, by General Qi Jiguang (1528–1587). There's also the *Record of Arms*, by Wu Shu (1611–1695), and *The Book of Chang-Style Martial Techniques*, by Chang Naizhou (1724–1783). There are slim pickings in between these important works until the mid-nineteenth century.

Toward the end of the nineteenth century, a prolific period of martial art research and writing can be seen in works by numerous authors, including Li Cunyi (1847–1921), Sun Lutang (1861–1933), Chen Weiming (1881–1958), Dong Xiusheng (1882–1939), Tang Hao (1887–1959), Jiang Rongqiao (1891–1974), Chen Ziming (b. ?–1951), Wan Laisheng (1903–1995), and others. So, from the mid-nineteenth century we can find some good references on Chinese martial arts. The writers usually focused on specific styles, particularly *xingyi, bagua, taiji, mizongquan*, Shaolin boxing, and Chinese wrestling, as well as the specific use of weapons, such as the spear, straight sword, and saber.

A Recently Discovered Martial Arts Manuscript

The story behind this discovery starts in June 2000, when two scholars from the University of Macau's Department of Philosophy and Religious Studies traveled to the Vatican to conduct a one-year research project on the Jesuit missionaries who were assigned to posts in China. The missions started with the founding of the Society of Jesus, whose member priests are called Jesuits. A co-founder, Francis Xavier (1506–1552), led the way to Asia for other Jesuits. From the time of Xavier's death to 1800, a total of 920 Jesuits participated in the China mission.

The Jesuits were highly educated, having studied in major academic institutes in Germany, Poland, Italy, France, Austria, Portugal, Spain, and elsewhere. Their work took them over much of Asia, crossing even remote areas such as Tibet and Nepal. Only a few were allowed to live and work in Beijing, including Johann Adam Schall von Bell (1591–1666) and Jean Joseph Marie Amiot (1718–1793). The stellar person among all the Jesuits to serve in China was Matteo Ricci (1552–1610), a genius with a photographic mind. Ricci and a number of other notable Jesuits were buried in Beijing at the Zhalan Cemetery.

The scholars from Macau had specific objectives in researching the Western contributions that the Jesuits made to China during their years in service. The Jesuit influence was truly great, especially in the sciences. Many translations were made, allowing the spread of Western thought. Topics and items introduced included medicine, mathematics, astronomy, cartography, hydraulics, geography, musical instruments, and artwork. Likewise, Jesuit work brought Europeans a new vision of the richness of Chinese history and culture.

One artist became very famous for the artworks he produced painting at the imperial court of three emperors— the Kangxi (1654–1722), Yongzheng (1678–1735), and Qian-long (1711–1799). His name was Lang Shining (1688–1766), and he held the status of official court painter. He painted many traditional themes such as flowers, animals, and landscapes. What fascinates those interested in martial arts are his works showing emperors, empresses, military campaigns, weapons, and warriors. He was also known for his architectural designs in the Old Summer Palace amid imperial gardens.

To this day, many educated Chinese are aware of Lang Shining's artworks. However, many do not know that his birth name was Giuseppe Castiglione (1688–1766)—and he was an Italian Jesuit. He designed Western-style buildings, which were constructed in 1747. In 1860, during the Second Opium War, European troops looted them and turned the magnificent buildings into rubble. Many of his paintings remain intact. They show his unique talent in blending Western and Chinese styles of painting. The paintings certainly look Chinese, but there is something different. Something captivating. The brush techniques of the Renaissance add a vibrancy of color and light, often with a perspective that is unordinary for the time.

While at the Vatican Library, the scholars from Macau thoroughly studied all writings and artifacts dealing with Castiglione. Most of the documents were in Italian and Latin. One folder that caught their eye contained many papers almost entirely in Chinese script. They weren't written in Castiglione's hand. Topics in the papers certainly dealt much with painting, philosophy, and religion. Among these were pages on martial arts. What a surprise! Who wrote these pages? Why did Castiglione have them?

After Castiglione died in Beijing, his personal items were sent to the Jesuit mother church, the Church of Gesù in Rome. Items dealing with Castiglione's work were eventually placed in the Vatican's Special Collections. Today much is in digital format. All personal items that were transported from China were to be given to his family in Milan. However, the folder with papers in Chinese script was inadvertently kept in Rome.

The Author and the Significance of the Text

How did Giuseppe Castiglione come into possession of this folder of Chinese writings? The scholars from Macau were quick to decipher from the Chinese text that the author befriended Castiglione due to their mutual love of painting and philosophy. The scholars from Macau presumed that

Castiglione had borrowed the folder of writings to read. Because Yang died less than a year before Castiglione's own passing, the papers remained in the hands of his Jesuit friend.

Details extracted from the documents provide insights. The author's name was Yang Mingbin (c. 1664–1765), from Song Village, which is located in Sheqi County in the southwestern side of Henan Province. Besides being a court painter, apparently Yang had mastered another art as well—a martial art, some hybrid of combatives he embodied from his studies with masters from the surrounding areas. Song Village is about 150 miles from the Shaolin Temple, 200 miles from Chen Village, and 155 miles from Wudang Mountain. Yang's first teacher, Du Xiayou, had been the head of the Song Village militia. In Yang's notes, he mentions friends who were martial art masters, including Chen Shanzhi of Chen Village. He also was in close contact with Chang Naizhou, whose writings reflect the thoughts and principles associated with taijiquan.

In Beijing, those who knew Yang only thought of him as a painter. His father and grandfather were leading figures in their home village. Their positions allowed Yang to pursue academic studies, painting, and martial art training with superb instructors. Since Yang was introverted, he focused on painting for a living and shared his combat knowledge and abilities with only his very closest friends. After his initial introduction to Castiglione as a painter, their friendship grew deeper through philosophical discussions revealing their kindred spirits. Castiglione became a close confidant.

Yang and Castiglione were not always intensely discussing mixing pigments, frontier wars, or the political topics of the day. As friends they had tea and chatted about their families, travels, and music, and shared a joke to break up the workday with some laughter. When Castiglione was telling his friend details about painting a portrait of the Qianlong Emperor's cherished "Fragrant Concubine," the usually prim and proper Jesuit whispered: "By accident, while she was changing for her portrait, I caught a glimpse of the beautiful woman fully nude. What a celestial vision!" Yang found this funny enough to note in his papers.

Left: Painting of Giuseppe Castiglione. Right: His painting of the Fragrant Concubine, *National Palace Museum, Taipei.* Public domain.

In Yang's writings, we find many clear expressions of how brush techniques parallel martial techniques. To wield either sword or brush requires a unity of mind, body, and spirit. Feeling each brush hair on paper requires profound sensitivity, much like the high skills exhibited in push-hands practice. Prerequisite to execution of movement is to be in a state of clear awareness, with a relaxed mind and body. Such themes are present in Yang's writings on both painting and martial arts.

Castiglione no doubt appreciated Yang's insights, which may have helped him with his artistic blending of East and West. It's certain too that Castiglione saw much of value in Yang's grasp of the martial side. Their days working together in Beijing were at the height of the Qing Dynasty (1644–1912). This dynasty was founded by the Northern Manchus, in part with the help of European technology used in casting cannons. Later, Johann Adam Schall von Bell was asked to build a foundry in Beijing to cast new cannons for the Qing forces, which were divided into the military/administrative system known as the Eight Banners. Manchu power created the imperial court atmosphere that allowed great cultural flourishing during Yang and Castiglione's time.

To fully appreciate Yang's writings, we see that he lived in a pivotal point in martial art history, one in which combative theory seems to have evolved, bringing the arts to a higher level of development. For example, Yang and Chang Naizhou were of one generation that preceded Chen Changxing (1771–1853), the teacher of Yang Luchan (1799–1872)—founder of Yang family taijiquan. How much influence did Yang Mingbin have on the development of Chinese martial arts? We can never know for sure, but it takes only a few anonymous masters of great talent to pass on knowledge and skills. As many masters went to great lengths to keep their arts secret, those who benefited were always few in number. Luckily, when we read Yang's text, we can better comprehend the depth of thought and related skills of the time.

When the University of Macau scholars finished their research project in July 2001, there was a question of what should be done with Yang Mingbin's writings. According to the Society of Jesus, personal possessions were to go to family. The scholars set out to find any of Yang's living relations. They had been prominent in his birthplace of Song Village in Henan. They were leaders in politics, military, and business. Government records listed some of the ancestors whose lineage could be traced to a centenarian named Yang Yingyin, who had died in 1990. He was the last living ancestor known to live in the village.

City officials helped check funeral records and learned that Yang Yingyin had one son, Yang Qingyu (1915–2002). He lived in Taiwan and served as a soldier in the National Revolutionary Army under the leadership of Generalissimo Chiang Kai-shek. The son had fought against the Communists and retreated to Taiwan in 1949 with the Nationalist Party. For decades the government imposed a political ban that kept anyone in Taiwan from visiting mainland China. However, in 1987 the ban was lifted, and Yang Qingyu finally got to visit Song Village in 1996.

Village officials saw that Yang Mingbin's writings would get to Yang Qingyu. When located, Yang was eighty-seven years old and had just started to decay in health. He felt great honor in receiving the writings and to learn of his special ancestor. It touched him greatly because he too was a lifelong martial art practitioner of the Shaolin and Yang taijiquan systems. Yang Qingyu was a well-known master in Taiwan, and he realized just how precious the writings were because the content showed that his ancestor's comprehension and skill level were far beyond his own.

During most of Yang Qingyu's years in Taiwan, he lived in Taipei. He later moved to the island's geographic center, to the town of Puli. He had some students and regularly taught monks at the Goddess of Mercy Buddhist temple, where he lived in the monastery. When nearly two million Nationalist Army troops retreated to Taiwan, Yang was one of the many men who remained unmarried. His close students were his closest "family."

Early in 2002, Yang Qingyu entered a hospital in Kaohsiung City. Knowing his time was short, he decided to give his most valuable possession—the original Yang Mingbin manuscript—to his main disciple, Huang Jingjie, who was his student from 1981 to his master's final days. One copy went to the Buddhist monastery. Huang decided to translate the manuscript into English with hopes that others would benefit in the understanding and practice of their Chinese martial art, especially for better health and longevity.

The folder with Yang Mingbin's writings contains over two hundred pages. More than half focus on painting. His brilliance shows in his profound grasp of Chinese and Western principles of aesthetics and technique—influenced in part by the Jesuits, and especially his friend Giuseppe Castiglione. Yang was inspired by Confucian, Buddhist, and Daoist thought, as well as Western Christianity and science. All were nurturing rivers from which he took refreshment. This was while the flourishing Qing Dynasty was at its cultural peak. Yang and Castiglione are seen as two of the best examples of true Renaissance men who were well informed in many areas of study.

Yang Mingbin was born gifted. His life was one dedicated to daily nurturing of mind, body, and spirit. The practice of martial arts was a perfect balance to his painting art. What he did painting, he did with the martial arts. His mind was always open to learning, testing, and practicing. As stated in a Chinese proverb:

> "What is accomplished in the mind
> is made known by the hand."

The following pages provide the translation of the mid-eighteenth–century writings of Yang Mingbin. The discovery of his manuscript is certainly of historical significance, particularly for anyone interested in the Chinese martial tradition and related aspects of physical culture, philosophy, and intercultural relations.

Yang had produced a series of short compositions on many topics. We have tried to present them here in a topical sequence. By expounding on combat practice, he presents the minutia of body movements, the sources of power, and the harmony of overall technique. Many of the principles applicable for combat transfer directly to martial art practice for nurturing health. In this collection, you will see the depth and breadth of martial arts as a vital component of Chinese culture at the high point of the imperial Qing Dynasty.

NOTE: The following section of Yang Mingbin's writings is arranged under sixty-four topics. These contain his personal thoughts relating to the martial arts. He has a wide perspective, looking at the broad spectrum of Chinese martial arts, rather than one limited by a specific style or location. In the attempt to translate as clearly as possible, the editor has used some modern names and terms rather than those of eighteenth-century China. In order to specify the romanization and meaning of some Mandarin words, brackets were used within sentences. Brackets were also used to provide extra details or when clarification of Yang's text seemed appropriate.

Yang Mingbin's Essays

Lingering Garden, Suzhou City.
Courtesy of Shutterstock, # 164159423.

Experiencing the Dao [Way] is my greatest joy. It is mysterious, moving through all things, hardly noticeable until in movement, like air we don't feel until it is a breeze. It is always here, flowing perfectly, and this is what brings pleasure while creating art or practicing martial arts.

For calligraphy and painting, the brush is the vital tool. It transmits the artist's mind, spirit, and energy. There is no hiding the artist's level of skill as the ink seeps into the paper. There's no way to make a correction afterward.

For martial arts, the body is the vital tool. It likewise reflects the individual's mind, spirit, and energy in each movement. The skill level is apparent. Concerning self-defense, a flaw can bring injury or death. There is no room for correction. Even if practiced solely as an exercise for nourishing health, the practice should conform to the correct principles to bring the desired effects. Regular practice improves one's overall physical and mental condition—soothing the nerves, maintaining flexibility and strength, encouraging blood and energy flow, and clarifying the mind. As Laozi wrote: "That which goes against the Dao comes to an early end."

The words for "calligraphy" [*shufa*] and "boxing" [*quanfa*] have the character *fa* in them, meaning "law" or "way." It is written by combining the characters for "water" and "go." It is the watercourse way, a natural movement. Painting and boxing have their own ways of being expressed. If done in accord with the Dao, the practitioner feels and sees perfection.

The character for fa carries the additional meaning of being moral, having a responsibility for discerning right from wrong. In Sanskrit, fa is called *dharma*—the spiritual way of Buddhism. A similar meaning is found in the character Dao, the Way of Daoism. The image is composed of a head topped by a warrior's hairstyle, signifying leadership, and a foot, signifying movement. The characters fa and Dao have profound meanings for a painter or martial artist who walks the Daoist path.

So, for painting, I arrange the "four treasures" on my desk: inkstone, ink stick, brush, and paper. My inkstone was created out of a rock from the Tao River in Gansu Province. Its innate surface patterns seem to play energetically while grinding the ink with water. While previously working mainly with oil soot ink, I have changed to pine soot ink, since it allows for more realism. This was inspired by my Jesuit friend, Giuseppe Castiglione. In commissioning the ink, I've prescribed a titch of selected powdered herbs to bring a healthy life to my paintings! The fragrance also is pleasing in the studio.

For both calligraphy and painting, I use Xuan paper from Anhui Province, as its smooth surface allows a very clean stroke, doesn't crease, and preserves well. But the brush is most important. There is a wide selection of brushes to use according to the task. Of course, there are sizes that vary from thin to thick. I choose the type of hair that is most appropriate for the job, usually from animals' tails, be it of wolf, sheep, civet, ox, rat, goat, weasel, horse, bull, or other. As with other professional calligraphers, I prefer brushes made with hair collected in the winter for their superb quality. The shafts I use are of simple bamboo. No mother-of-pearl inlay, ivory, or jade garnish for me. Just natural bamboo to give the best feel. My brushes are from Houdian Village in Shandong Province.

For martial arts, I devote time each day to practice in the secluded garden courtyard of my home. Unlike most courtyards in Beijing, I keep the central area pure dirt, rather than covered in stone. The texture of the dirt is slightly soft under my shoes, which provides a wonderful feel for the whole body, especially when landing from jumping maneuvers.

Along the courtyard walls are trees, which provide shade and protect the yard from winds, important as to not adversely affect the balance of the five internal bodily elements of fire, earth, wood, water, and metal. The trees are mostly pine, but there are a few willows, a silk tree, small bushes, and a variety of flowers. On one side is a tea pavilion where I sometimes meet with other martial artists and good friends. We can chat while leisurely sipping *lao ren cha* [tea for elders] and sample their fragrances and tastes, detecting the nuances of each wonderful tea.

The painting studio and the boxing courtyard are not just walled areas. They are sacred places for studying the Dao and forging the spirit. Entering these spaces, I leave the world of dust behind and wholeheartedly focus on what is being done on the paper or dirt ground. The body-mind is but a medium. Years of training allow the mind to see the task at hand and movement seems to commence, unbound by time. However, unlike brushwork, the effort in the courtyard rewards one in a layer of sweat.

How well can I express my intention through my brush or straight sword? Can I perform each movement perfectly and purposely, with no hesitation? This is the reason we have a boxing style named *xingyiquan* [form-intent boxing]. The mind creates form. As in the medical field, it is said: "Where the mind goes, the vital energy goes." As some adepts in the fighting arts advise, "Use mind; don't use muscle power."

So, there is work ahead for making steady improvement. In practice, we look not only to improve physical technique, but to polish the mind, which leads all movement. The mind is key, but a monkey-mind will only confuse and produce a low-level skill. A mirrorlike mind, calm and clear, is more suitable. The Dao of painting and the martial arts is a process of inner alchemy that changes the normal mode of thinking and moving.

Unity in Diversity

Each geographic area in the Middle Kingdom speaks its own dialect, produces its unique food products, and can be identified by clothing styles. Diversity within the land finds unity in a singular kingdom. Each area also developed its own uniquely identifiable martial art styles. The diversity of these fighting arts finds unity in the universal.

There are only so many ways to punch and kick. What accounts for the many differences we find in even the most basic of techniques, such as the punch? It is obvious that different levels of skill can be visually discerned. One method for grading skill level is to test techniques, such as a punching technique to break roof tiles. When practitioners of equal physical attributes attempt to break an object, many are not successful, some are, and a few can perform with extraordinary results. When these individuals punch, there are slight differences in their arm and hand positions, such as extension, muscle tension, and angle of attack. But there are more aspects to consider.

Upon closer observation, we notice these individuals use the whole body differently. What initiates the punch? Does it start with arm muscle, waist, or even in the feet? Do the shoulders and hips turn? There is a wide range of differences among individuals in how they physically perform a punch. Their skill level shows in the results of their breaking technique. However, the results are not only due to the physical structuring.

The mind's vision of technique plays heavily on the execution. If one believes tense musculature improves the ability to break a roof tile, the idea itself becomes embodied in the technique. The degree of tension can vary as countless other attributes do, such as variance in stance, chamber position, direction preference for stepping, and linear versus circular trajectory. When all such nuances are performed together repeatedly, the movement becomes habit. Habits create stylistic movements, and may later be given a name to distinguish the uniqueness as a specific style.

Practitioners have different reasons for studying a martial art. Soldiers must focus on weaponry and coordinated tactics to achieve their desired goal to maim or kill enemies. Peking opera actors need to portray stories from the stage to their audience. Street performers excite the crowd with dramatic displays. Others may be only concerned with practicing solo or in small groups to nurture their health. Some preserve secret family combative traditions in order to protect their homes and families. The variety of reasons for learning a martial art manifests in the spectrum of styles.

Particular styles emphasize specific techniques, such as joint locking, wrestling, kicking, striking, or throwing. A few styles are more encompassing. They may include standing and ground techniques, as well as weaponry—but the more facets included, the more study time is required. There is certainly great diversity in combative styles. Nevertheless, there is unity when these are perceived as variations on a universal art of combat that exists only in the imagination of the perfect art.

Artwork © by Feodor Tamarsky.

Inspiring Factors

Many arts are passed on from one generation to the next, such as painting, dance, music, and the healing arts. The reasons one may teach or study these arts affect how they are practiced. For example, music ranges from rustic folk to lofty imperial, associated with a variety of instruments. These musicians have very different backgrounds and intentions for performing. Likewise, we find a variety of martial art styles manifested.

Before the time of the Yellow Emperor [2697–2597 BCE], martial arts were developing for defense against human and animal attack. Over the centuries of dynastic change, martial arts evolved, including a vast variety of weapons. Today combative arts are found throughout the kingdom, including many family-based styles, as well as at the famous centers of Shaolin and Wudang.

The original combative purpose continues for the protection of villages and states, but there are many branches diverging from combative use. It is natural to maintain real fighting techniques in military training for use against outsiders, but to be somewhat more compassionate with locals in one's family neighborhoods. Philosophical influences took away many of the lethal aspects in favor of practicing for physical, mental, and spiritual development. With the mixing of Buddhist and Daoist exercise practices—such as *yijin changes* [muscle-tendon changes] and Hua Tuo's *wuqinxi* [five animal frolics]—many of the movements remained but practiced for health while knowledge of the original fighting applications was not included. Looking back over time, we see the mixing of martial arts and health exercises occurring at a growing frequency. This finds parallel in the increasing number of texts and verbal descriptions used by masters to explain the combative movements by utilizing traditional medical theory dealing with meridians and energy flow.

Left to right: tiger, bear, deer, bird, ape. Illustrations of the Five Animals from *The Cinnabar Book of Longevity*, a text composed in the Ming Dynasty (1368–1644) by Gong Juzhong. Courtesy of the Wellcome Collection.

Martially inspired movements are incorporated into many forms of entertainment, from street shows to opera. They certainly create excitement for the onlooker and emphasize the conflicts present in any good theatrical production or temple dances used to ward off evil. As in stage dramas and temple celebrations, some secular dance forms include martial techniques in their repertoire.

From the above, we see that some martial art styles retain their original lethal purpose while others do not. The variety of manifestations is fine, but to comprehend the full richness of martial traditions requires that we concentrate on the arts as they were originally developed.

Levels of Skill

Calligraphy students can never forget their first lesson: writing the character for the number one [a simple left to right stroke], over and over again. The second and third lessons are more of the same. When they are able to write it with a fair degree of smoothness and balance, they can move on to the number two [two parallel left-to-right strokes]. A good martial arts teacher starts in similar fashion, with the basics.

After practicing martial arts for some months, it may dawn on the student that making progress is difficult, requiring much more time and effort to reach mastery than initially expected. After ten years' work, the student may feel accomplished, until crossing hands with a better master. It may take thirty or forty years to approach the higher levels of skill. In reality, the road to mastery is infinite.

What are the differences in skill levels from beginner to advanced? One indicator is the number of techniques learned, from lower to higher, indicating an increase in knowledge. Here we must keep in mind that quality is more important than quantity. All practitioners exhibit their individual abilities as a unique personal expression, regardless of the purpose and use of the arts, such as in street exhibitions, flowery shows, or solo routine practice. How skills manifest is related to purpose.

When focusing on the arts as true combat forms, additional

factors need to be considered. Is the execution of these techniques done with efficiency, accuracy, and power? If done in actual combat, is the timing of the movement optimal? The attributes equated with good technique become better understood with experience. But some attributes are much more abstruse because they involve the invisible workings of the mind.

While facing an opponent who is about to attack, a high-level master is so aware at the start of the attack that he simultaneously executes an effective counter. A practitioner at a lesser level of skill, even knowing five thousand techniques, will hesitate or defend with an ineffective counter. Just knowing techniques is not enough. Thinking and planning how to respond is not enough. All the physical abilities required to perfect techniques are not enough. The technical side works in conjunction with the mental side, reaching deep into one's intuition in pursuit of martial perfection. Any movement guided by intuition is oiled by a clear mind and calm emotions. No room for fear or hate to disrupt the flow. The mental state is more important than the physical.

A large percentage of martial art practitioners represent the beginner level, a much smaller percentage the midlevel, and a very small percentage is advanced. We have an idea of where we place along this continuum by comparing our martial skills with those of others—the skills that include the workings of muscles, bones, joints, nerves, and mind integrated into technique. There is another level beyond advanced, one that is transcendental, a true mastery rarely witnessed. These adepts are as rare as the unicorn and the dragon.

The Paradox of Movement

Toss a peach to another person. It seems ridiculous to ask, "How is this action done?" We simply lob it forward. Upon close observation, we notice the arm moves backward before throwing forward.

Jump up, as onto the top of a low wall. The body does not

simply move upward, but first sinks downward to get enough spring in the legs to rise higher.

Slowly step to the left, and you'll notice that first shifting to the right foot is what allows the left foot to be free to step.

In these cases, we see that the desired movement is initiated in the opposite direction from the actual intended direction. Move the arm back in order to move it forward. Sink before jumping. Shift right before stepping left.

In Daoism, it is said, "One produces two, two produce three, and three produce all things." The hint is that yin and yang bring about movement. In one is the seed of the other. Martial art techniques spring from the oscillation between yin and yang. This is the secret in learning ten thousand techniques.

Bathing in Stillness

Movement is the essence of martial arts. Regarding self-defense, the ability to move well is a matter of life and death. Efficient movement also nourishes the body, improving or maintaining good health that ensures the longevity of the tortoise. This is so important that we must become aware of the attributes of both clumsy and efficient movements, which will then allow us to distinguish the stages of potential development. Thus the kinetic quality can gradually improve and progress is guaranteed.

To embody the Dao in movement is to move naturally. How can we accomplish this? By making each movement perfect, forcing every part of the body to be in a position we think is correct? If done in this fashion, we are trying to force the body to be natural, which is a contradiction. To move naturally is to let the body move naturally and only through practice can we discover how the body efficiently functions.

Some people who try to stand on one leg holding a static posture have no balance and fall immediately. Others can hold the posture for a short time before tipping, while very few can

9

hold the posture for an hour without wavering. If we can't even hold a static posture properly, it isn't possible to set out in motion. We learn to walk before running.

At the first stage of instruction, many masters start students with static postures, such as *standing post* and *rooster stands on one leg*. For many, these appear to be very boring practice methods, useless for serious combat. But when closely observed, these methods offer a way to become aware of balance, relaxation, and the connection between body and mind—necessary for improving every type of fighting technique.

While standing, the muscles fatigue and the practitioner subconsciously lets go of unnecessary tensions, little by little over time. Leaning requires muscle tension and strains the joints, making static standing difficult. One quickly learns that less of a tilt makes standing easier. The body finds that being balanced is the most comfortable position. Over days and months of practice, one becomes more and more aware of many subtle changes. Deeper relaxation and improved balance make holding postures more comfortable. After being able to comfortably hold static postures, the student is then ready to learn martial movements.

Standing on One Leg

While standing on one leg and holding the posture for five minutes, martial art practitioners often believe they are totally relaxed and balanced. The following offers a test that helps for observing and discovering if there are any remaining bodily tensions.

Stand on one leg with your knee slightly bent, as in *rooster stands on one leg*. Both arms can be in the *standing post* position, as if you're embracing a large tree—or you can leave one arm up and the other down, like *stork spreads wings*. Yet another option is simply to allow both arms to hang down and remain limp. Relax as much as possible. If you are very relaxed, it should be easy to maintain your balance during the minutes of holding.

Mentally scan the body for tensions from the head down, especially the shoulders. Finally, are there any muscular movements in the sole of the foot? If there are, then slight muscle twitches are making microadjustments to keep the body balanced. The more you are off balance, the more your foot will twitch. Being off balance, even a little, causes tension —and any tension can cause you to be off balance. Remaining attentive to these subtleties, you will gradually improve until the twitching is nearly imperceptible. At this advanced stage of relaxation and balance, you will no doubt feel the energy of the earth stimulating the bubbling well [the kidney 1 acupoint] in the middle of the sole of your foot.

One Step at a Time

We have numerous stationary practices, some even lying down! But, as martial artists, we want to move. By practicing the standing postures—on one leg or both—we develop skills in sensing and awareness. These will greatly help us to learn the intricate movements of any martial system.

Now, we start to move by looking closely at how we step. It doesn't matter in which direction, as the principles will be the same. The familiar principles we wish to maintain in movement are balance and relaxation. Go ahead: slowly take one step forward with the left foot. How did you do it? Many lift the foot and quickly set it down because they are off balance. If not done with some speed, they would fall.

Try again, but this time much slower. You'll feel it is impossible to lift the left foot without first shifting all the weight onto the right leg. Shifting allows one to keep balance throughout, gradually emptying one leg (*yin*), while making the other full (*yang*).

After shifting on the right leg, make a large step with the left. How did you place the foot out so far, making a wide stance? There are two ways. Did you start to step while leaning forward at the same time? If you did, then there was a loss of balance, which causes an acceleration of speed, and then requires tensions to catch the movement. This is a loss of principles. There is another way to make the step without losing the principles. The secret is to simultaneously sink into the right leg as you step out with the left leg. The more you sink, the wider the step and resulting stance. You can maintain balance and relaxation throughout the movement.

From static posture practice comes the first step, leading to routines. Some masters instruct disciples to practice routines in a slow, even tempo, while sensing for any tension or leaning. In Chen family taijiquan, a number of masters teach disciples to first move slowly, and later to move fast. They first concentrate on embodying the yin principle in routines. When the mind and body can maintain this principle in practice, the disciple gradually adds the yang principle. The boxing then manifests taiji, the harmonious flow of yin and yang in movement.

Slow versus Fast

In order to learn a martial art well, leading masters tell their students to begin by moving slowly. This gives ample time for the students to closely observe themselves in movement. They have opportunities to discover subtleties that hinder or facilitate their movements, such as muscle tensions, balance, and alignment. They learn to work with gravity and how techniques connect with the ground.

There are benefits of stationary-stance training and stepping slowly into stances. These and similar practices teach students the fundamentals of movement and technique. It is difficult enough to keep our balance and remain relaxed while moving slowly, but what happens when we gradually increase the speed of movements?

Through mindful practice we can gain knowledge of the role physics plays in the leisurely mode of training. As practice tempo increases, physical conditions change. For example, when a standing archer shoots on a calm day, there is a smooth trajectory to the posted target. If the target is moving, as a running rabbit, he needs to shoot ahead of it to hit the mark. If an archer is galloping on a horse and shoots on a windy day, there are even more factors to consider.

While standing still, the spine will be plumb vertical. When the body moves with any speed, the spine should not be held stiff. The spine, legs, and arms are like bows of the body, each flexing when appropriate with the ability to absorb or emit energy in combat.

Just because a student can perform slowly, with great balance, relaxation, and flexibility, that does not mean he or she will be able to move well when speed is required. If we seek to move with speed, we enter another realm of studies and practice. The earlier, slow practices have prepared us for this more advanced level. We will eventually be able to move quickly, yet remain relaxed and balanced. Techniques we have habituated by practicing slowly and repeatedly will not require much thinking to perform faster.

Students strive to gain awareness of the many facets relating to mind and body, details that occur while practicing at a slow tempo. Practicing at faster tempos brings a deluge of additional factors to consider. Perhaps the greatest difficulty is in perceiving elements that hide from our normal view. For this reason, we seek the blessing: to become aware of what is usually overlooked.

Magic Knuckles

The Daoist Zhuangzi presents many stories about how the actions of people reflect their affinity with the Dao. He highlights various skill levels as displayed by those in common occupations. For example, butchers in a meat market need to sharpen their knives to cut through carcasses. Some need to sharpen their knives when each new carcass arrives, while others have no need to do so until after trimming a few carcasses. Still yet, one butcher never needed to sharpen his knife at all: he wielded his blade through the spaces in between bone joints. Such mastery of technique is to what martial artists aspire.

Fighting techniques seem innumerable when considering all forms of strikes, kicks, locks, breaks, throws, jumps, deflections, blocks, escapes, and stances. And here we are only looking at bare-hand combat. How to execute the vast repertoire of techniques with mastery? Each technique has differences and similarities with other techniques. If we look closely at how one technique is performed, we can extrapolate insights for any other technique.

Let's look at a basic punch made in a ready front stance, and let's say the intention is to break a roof tile that is braced in a wooden stand. If ten individuals attempt this strike, they will all show some differences in how they punch. Their skill levels are not the same. In most cases, they will rely on speed, power, and muscle tension to make a successful break. Some prepare for this through methods that callous their knuckles. Some lift weights and exercise to strengthen their muscles. It is no surprise that they can break the tiles. Then we see a relatively thin person with little apparent strength break a tile with a seemingly effortless strike. We can look at just one feature of this technique that will hint at the many small but highly significant parts that make up the whole technique.

Pull each finger of the right hand into a formed fist and chamber it at the waist. Left arm and leg at front. Shoulders angled, aligned with the hips, weight on the back leg, knee slightly bent. Simultaneously, as the strike is made, the back leg straightens, the hips turn, and the arm flies toward the tile. Pieces fall to the ground.

In this technique, varied degrees of tension are present

throughout the body. How much tension is necessary? Great tension certainly feels powerful, and it seems to support and add power to the fist. However, all the tensions from the heel to the hand will not make the knuckles any harder than the natural bone and cartilage.

Some rely on tensions to prevent injury to themselves, which is especially possible when the technique is done with poor form. For example, a slightly bent wrist can be sprained or even broken from a single punch. Alignment is a key factor in all techniques, for safety as well as power. Important for the punch is to get the knuckles to arrive at the tile with speed. Tensions actually can slow the movement, so more muscle power is necessary to break through the target. Proper alignment and fluid, relaxed movement allow you to execute the technique with a free flow of inner energy at optimal speed. Such conditions are necessary requirements for any technique.

Split the Globe

For defending or attacking, one's body needs to move quickly and with ease in any direction. The ability to move in this manner involves aspects of flexibility and alignment of the skeletal and muscular systems. Well-coordinated martial artists appear to move effortlessly, usually not in all possible directions, but in many. Others show various degrees of strain, which hinders their movements and places them at risk during combat. Thus, having fewer tensions in the body makes a better quality of movement possible.

One way to understand how tensions can show up in the body is to visualize the many moving parts, especially involving the joints. For example, it is common enough that one may turn the shoulder far left while freezing the legs in a static stance. This can strain muscles and vertebrae.

Think of a ball made of down feathers encased in cloth. Place one hand underneath and one on top. Hold the bottom tightly so it can't move. Then slowly try to turn the top. It should show at least some slight movement, and with more force, it will tear the ball. Great force can simply tear it in half. This tear results from stress made when one part moves and another either moves slower or not at all. However, when the whole ball moves as one, there is no tension.

When practicing combat techniques with any speed, beginners must give great attention to the potential of strain so as not to cause injury. For example, there are common attacks where one advances with a two-step movement while the body is spinning 360 degrees. It is extremely important that when the first foot hits the ground with the heel, the foot and leg continue as the body turns, pivoting on the heel. As the second foot hits the ground, it must do the same. If the foot lands on the ground flat and freezes while the rest of the body turns, damage will occur in the knee.

If some parts of the body are strongly held firm while other parts move quickly, the fighting technique will certainly be considered as low skill level, dangerous to the practitioner. A wise person will constantly strive to find any body area that strains even a little during practice and try to alleviate it. Any martial technique should be executed with the flow of the whole body, so no strain can manifest.

Straight at an Angle

Many strikes and pushes are made straight ahead, especially when practicing techniques with a partner. The very thought that these techniques are directed forward is a cause for many inexperienced practitioners to embed a fault. We can look at a forward two-hand push as an example.

Beginners who try to push by using their fingers learn a quick, painful lesson: the fingers are too weak to withstand much pressure. The most common push with the hand is done by making contact with the palm. If you are new to martial art practice, you might make the mistake of pushing with the arms directly in front of your shoulders. This width is excessive. If the person being pushed turns even slightly, your left and right arms become unbalanced and lose the intended effect.

A point to make here is that, although your instinct may be to push straight ahead, you should direct your hands to move in angles toward the opponent's center. This forms a triangle. If we imagine your shoulders as two points of a triangle, the third would be a focal point just behind the opponent. Compared to the straight-ahead push, the triangular push is more stable—and therefore more effective.

The palm positions are also affected. If your palms face directly forward while your arms are angled toward the opponent's center, tensions result in the wrists, making them susceptible to injury. Since the arms are slightly angled toward the opponent's center, so should the palms be angled. The outer sides of the palms will make first contact and provide the most stable alignment for pushing. Experiment with this angular push to find the natural alignment for comfort and high effectiveness.

Pushing and Punching Distance

What distance should one be from an opponent for an optimally effective push or punch? Reaching toward an opponent, a new practitioner often starts at arm's length. This works, but it is not a very effective method, especially if your weight is mostly in the front foot.

For practice, place the instep of your right foot directly in front of your opponent's lead foot. Shift all your weight into the right foot, sinking into the leg while stepping with your left foot to the side and behind the opponent's lead foot. Lightly place both hands against your opponent's rib cage. In order to do this, you must be very close to the opponent, and your palms will be facing forward, elbows pointing down. Keep most of your weight on your back leg. If you are training by yourself, you can get the same feeling by pushing against a large tree trunk for practice.

Pressing lightly against the resistant surface will allow you to feel the physical connections running from the back foot; through the leg, torso, and shoulders; and into the arms and hands. In such a posture, the power of the push should come from the back leg, not from the arms. The hands and arms merely make contact while the legs emit power.

This type of push is not force against force. To be effective, it is executed while the other person is in retreat, which is usually just after an attack has been neutralized. There is no clash of forces. Rather it is an adding of force to the opponent's retreat. The only people I've met who have mastered the intricacies illustrated in the above example are a few reclusive Daoists in the Wudang Mountains. Their touch is as light as a gosling's feather, yet they emit the force of a lightning bolt.

Footwork as Brushwork

There are written records of immortals who can float on clouds, run across the surface of ponds, and walk over snow yet leave no trail. I've been fortunate to meet a few Daoist recluses in the Wudang Mountains, and I can understand why these myths began. I can assure you that these people are mortals, but with exceptional mental, physical, and spiritual gifts. Their fighting skills appear to exude the paranormal, but they sweat and fart as any normal folk. The clouds they float on through the sky may simply be their own gas vapors.

And float they do. Their martial movements glide with grace, accuracy, and speed, seemingly unhampered by physical laws. Their smoothness, variations in speed, and ability to change directions at will give the appearance of a master calligrapher wielding an ink brush. Their physical movements appear to be more of liquid than bone.

When writing characters or painting a landscape, we hold the brush upright. The bamboo shaft is the spine, and the brush leaves its tracks. So soft and flexible are the brush hairs that they immediately convey the intentions, even the spirit, of the writer. Such ideas are conveyed in the *Manual of the Mustard Seed Garden*, a brilliant work commissioned by Shen Xinyou. I am euphoric seeing how the movements of a brush tip find parallel in the foot and leg movements of my Daoist hermit teachers. I'll try to write down the parallels I see between these arts.

First, like the softest of goat hair, the feet and ankles of the Daoist masters are relaxed at ease, capable of moving smoothly at will, in any direction on a compass. For calligraphers, the vertical directions in relation to the paper are just as important as the martial artists' lifting and setting feet in relation to the ground. Like the brush, the feet are guided by intention, unhampered in any way. While the calligrapher creates characters, the martial artist spontaneously creates the footwork of combat techniques.

Lowering the brush toward paper, the tip—just one or two hairs—will touch first, then more according to the desired thickness. With variations in directional movements to make any stroke, the hairs move at the artist's will, reflecting the mind's intent. Lowering the leg toward the ground, the toes—perhaps just the largest—touch first. Then the rest of the foot incrementally meets the ground. The ankle and knee act as hinges, bending and easing contact with the ground, especially helpful when landing from jumping maneuvers.

Courtesy of
Shutterstock.
ID: 294607298

Lifting reverses the process. For the brush, as the calligrapher slowly lifts the handle, more and more hairs leave the paper, until the last hair at the tip loses contact. Raising the leg is similar to raising the brush handle. The knee starts upward, lifting the heel and finally the toes.

The feet barely leave the ground when moving in any direction. Often they skim over the ground surface, sensing the terrain as the body makes transitions between postures. On a smooth dirt surface, foot patterns remain—showing linear or curving actions according to the requirements of the whole body movement.

When one leg is bearing weight, the other foot may be lightly set on the ground, as in *play lute*, with the heel on the ground, or in *stork spreads wings*, with the ball of the foot on the ground. In these types of stances, the front leg should be relaxed enough that when the waist and shoulders move left or right, there is also movement in the foot. This will leave a swivel mark on the ground, much like the mark left when the calligrapher turns the shaft and the brush hairs follow. Thus, the foot patterns on the ground surface will leave every type of brush movement: horizontal, vertical, dotted, curved, rising, falling, turning, hooked, and various combinations.

Remember that brush movements contain simultaneous actions, such as a slow downward movement letting the brush slightly touch the paper but moving as more of the brush presses wider, circling and lifting for a thin line moving into another direction, then heavily downward into a perfectly elongated line. All such brush movements are easily seen when done with a "dry brush" technique—when the brush is not so wet—so many individual hair markings are visible on the paper.

The parallels between brush and foot movements hint at the qualities needed to make them. One is great sensitivity. A good calligrapher can feel the paper even when only one hair of the brush touches it. A good martial artist feels the terrain as well as any pressure that touches the legs. One must also be relaxed so either brush or leg can be moved with dexterity. For self-defense, such qualities allow many effective leg techniques. At the same time, knowing that stiff legs are easily attacked, cultivating sensitivity and dexterity in the legs provides measures of safety.

Shoulder to Shoulder

The shoulders factor largely into fighting techniques. Defensive and offensive movements extend from the shoulders to the fingertips. We often think of the hands and elbows as the primary tools, but the shoulders are also used independently. For example, they may function as points of leverage or be used for striking and pushing.

The shoulders are anchored to the body by its skeletal design, and the inherent width between them manifests in a fount of natural techniques. When the shoulders turn side to side, relaxed arms will move side to side. The distance between the hands varies some, but basically keep a distance in sync with the shoulders. An example here would be defending against a left-hand strike. As the attacker steps in to throw, turn slightly to the right, and the arms follow. Then, by turning to the left, the shoulders turn, and the arms follow to curve upward and circle left, landing on the attacker's left wrist and elbow. Notice the natural shoulder-width distance between your hands while they are hanging down. It matches the distance between the attacker's wrist and elbow. The defender's arm positions are intrinsically effective for defense.

This is a basic rollback type of technique used in all styles. Important here is noting that the arms are not tensed with an attempt to block. There is a natural flow of the movement, actually emanating from the waist through the shoulders, then to the hands. The arms aren't forced to move directly to the oncoming punch. First they circle under and away from the attack, and then they circle up to meet it. Initially, it seems unnatural to move away from the oncoming attack, but once you master this technique, it feels extremely easy and highly practical.

Another example should help illustrate this shoulder-to-arm movement. This can be seen in the rising-arms defense, often used when an attacker reaches in to grab your coat collars or neck. One defense could be simply to move back a step out of the attacker's reach. If your hands are resting at the sides or in front of the body, there is no need to lift the arms forcibly to block! Keep your hands just where they are while initiating the step backward. As your body moves away from the hands, the hands will appear to be rising on their own. The backward movement starts the forearms moving upward to meet the attack. As the arms freely follow your body movement, they move in a curve, first upward to meet the underside of the attacker's arms, then toward your own shoulders. From here, a follow-up technique would be used as desired.

When you stand in a stationary position, the arms inherently hang at the same width as the shoulders. With the two examples discussed above, we can see and feel how the arms naturally follow the shoulders, initiated from the waist. This is the most comfortable position from which movements can commence. When you maintain relaxation in the shoulder joints, the arms maneuver according to intent, offering safety to the joints and ease of technique.

Practical Techniques, Proper Forms

Many students begin to learn a martial art by imitating their teacher's movements. The quality of any movement or technique depends greatly upon the inborn physical and mental abilities of the student, which develop over time, especially through martial art training. The student will often think he is perfectly copying the teacher's movements, when, in fact, he's making numerous mistakes. No matter how many techniques or forms he memorizes simply by watching, quality will be lacking. The body structure will not be precise, with flaws appearing in hand and foot positions, and tensions hampering the gestures and straining the body.

How can students make refinements? Of course, if the master is willing to point out mistakes and make corrections, students will improve. After years of work, they may perform a technique or routine beautifully. The progress is noticeable. At this critical stage, students may be motivated to give public performances, and their movements may become more flowery and entertaining, on the cusp of becoming gymnastic exercises. This is fine, but there are additional steps necessary for the mastery of any combat art.

Martial art styles embody a great variety of forms. This is similar to languages having lengthy vocabularies. When someone speaks a totally foreign language, we hear only unintelligible sounds. The language can only reveal deep meaning if the listener comprehends the full significance of each word, including the various definitions and context. This analogy applies to the martial arts as well. To really understand what a master may show, it is necessary to know what each movement means and its potential uses. Therefore, simply copying a movement, or imitating a word, is not enough. It is necessary to dive deeper to understand the martial applications. Applications give meaning to the movements.

According to tradition, a master usually chooses three loyal and talented students as disciples to receive the deepest teachings. With them, methods of instruction become more hands-on, at a more challenging skill level. Two people practice the techniques, one attacking and one defending. Initially, they practice slowly, but over the course of months, they speed up, and the training becomes more realistic. Scenarios then often include multiple attackers.

Practicing applications allows the student to learn exactly how and why each technique is done. In so doing, the placement of the whole body structure, especially noticed in hand and foot positions, gives meaning to the form. The understanding and feeling become part of the practitioner to the point that, even when movements are done solo, the body and mind can move precisely, as if done in actual combat mode.

If the student does not fully understand the applications, solo practice embodies deficiencies, which, in turn, become habits.

The Attack Makes the Defense

There is often talk about martial art masters who uphold stern ethical beliefs that guide their practice and the teaching of their fighting arts. One guideline is that a superior person should not be an aggressor who throws the first strike. There are other good reasons for not being the aggressor. A master who senses an eminent attack will recognize it from the start and be able to avoid the charge while simultaneously countering.

The concept of self-defense is one for the protection of ourselves—and others. We protect ourselves from any type of attack. An experienced fighter benefits in knowing that when attacked, the aggressor creates openings at the same time, which can be exploited. For example, a punch toward the head welcomes a counter to the body below the attacking arm. The attack always opens doors to be entered with a counterattack. So, there is an advantage for the defender in opportunities to counter as well as in the timing of the technique.

There can be many different responses to a particular attack, mainly reflecting the skill level of the defender. A low-level response would be to put great effort into blocking and then some hesitation for how to counterattack. A higher-level response would be to smoothly neutralize the attack (yin) and simultaneously launch an effective counter (yang). The latter response requires a mastery of techniques, uninhibited by physical tensions and a muddled mind. Mental training and preparation are even more important than physical training. Only with this groundwork will you be able to truly have the higher skills for defense. With the technical tools and a polished mind, you will be relaxed and spontaneously flow to meet any combative situation.

How does an attack create the defense? We can analyze

one technique to see what it can teach us. If a person approaches to push on your right shoulder with his left hand, your response may be to tense with the desire to withstand the push, then to counter. By tensing, the push will surely disrupt your body, freezing your arms from any natural counter. However, by being relaxed, the push would simply turn you, and you can remain in balance. By turning right, you neutralize the push. If you are not tense, the energy from the attacker's push goes to your right shoulder, then directly to your left shoulder. This simultaneously causes your left arm to swing upward, to the outside of the attacker's left arm, near his elbow. At the same time, your right hand can swing up to pin the attacker's left wrist to your right shoulder. By not resisting the attacker's push, his force will lead him forward, and he will become off balance. You can then reverse movement by turning left, easily throwing the attacker away to your left side. The attacker has created your counter.

Sources of Tension

A professional dancer's movements seem to defy gravity, with smooth, flowing gestures of effortless grace. The calligrapher's brush moves swiftly over the paper, creating each character of a poem in perfect balance and harmony. Any tension occurring during the execution of movement shows the loss of balance and shaky form. Martial movements often exhibit the same faults, which are largely caused by tensions in the body.

From where do these tensions arise? For the martial artist, the main cause of tension is fear. Fear of injury can dominate the mindset. It is easy to understand how fear arises in these settings, especially when weapons are involved. If you know you possess only low-level fighting skills, the terror of combat can cripple your movements. More experienced fighters show less fear and tension. They are more capable of moving swiftly and accurately as needed. They do not freeze or hesitate.

Fear and its resulting tensions also appear in solo practice, such as when performing the routines created to preserve a style's repertoire of techniques. With no apparent danger around, why would fear and tensions invade the body? In this case, fear comes when one is unsure a movement can be executed properly. This is the fear of failing. We fear losing balance during *rooster stands on one leg*—or falling head over heels while sinking down to a low posture. To maintain an upright position, we often resort to tensions as we fight the feeling of going off balance. By being in balance, there is no fear of falling or any need to be tense.

People have different theories regarding how to perform techniques most effectively. Many will prove effective, but there's no doubt that some methods are better than others. A major theme of debate is just how much or how little tension should be utilized in applications. High-level skills appear effortless, with minimal tension and excellent results. Lower-level skills show some amount of tensions necessary to get the technique to work. Whenever someone with low-level skills attempts to do a technique in a more relaxed fashion, it will fail. He may blame the method, ignoring that he simply has not mastered the skill well enough to be effective.

We need to look closely at the effect tensions have on martial practice and also health. Bodily tensions occurring while fighting actually hamper the potential speed possible in movement. Tensions also make the body more susceptible to injuries, especially in the elbows and knees.

Those who know how to use muscular strength to force technique will move accordingly. Those who can use more relaxed methods will use those methods. The amount of tension used is in proportion to what they believe is necessary. The only way to improve one's skills is to keep experimenting, practicing, and learning. Test constantly. In this way, what you believe does not work today may prove to be a superior method later.

The sage Laozi wrote:

> Nothing in the world is softer and weaker than water.
> Yet, to attack the hard and strong,
> Nothing surpasses it.
> Nothing can take its place.
> The weak overcomes the strong.
> The soft overcomes the hard.
> Everybody in the world knows this,
> Still nobody makes use of it.

Laozi knew that many cannot clear tensions from the body and maintain calm. There are many who claim that tensions will dissipate by practicing methods such as deep breathing, Daoist yoga, hot baths, and chanting. These methods may provide a period of relaxation and comfort, but they do not last. They are temporary fixes because these are superficial means that do not reach the heart of the matter. The tensions we see and feel are only the physical results brought on by the mind. Those seeking to improve their martial skills are obliged to nourish mental awareness, perhaps with the help of meditation practices for developing their inner vision and discovering the origins of tension.

Better Vision

Even from afar, eagles spot the smallest of animals that humans cannot notice at such a distance. In the darkness, owls catch mice that are imperceptible to any human in a similar setting. While a man has limited frontal vision, a sheep sees forward and to both sides simultaneously. When discussing martial arts, the truly accomplished martial art masters see more subtleties in fighting techniques than do others.

Watching a highly skilled master perform a short solo routine, the common person sees three movements: (1) the arms moving in circles, (2) a low left kick, and (3) a turn to face the opponent in a guard stance. It is impossible to miss the great speed and use of a variety of body parts employed in the combat forms.

Although witnessing the same practice routine, one with more experience in the martial arts notices more: 1) the arms spin like a windmill to deflect a punch. (2) A left-hand strike is executed, followed by a left kick to the opponent's knee. (3) A 180-degree turn is made to move into the opponent, pushing him to the ground.

What does a master imagine in this scenario? (1) An attacker reaches out with both hands, so the defender quickly shifts to his right while turning his waist first to the right then to the left. This effortlessly circles his arms to deflect both the opponent's arms to the left. Continuing the circular movement, the defender shifts left. He turns his waist to the right while striking out with the left open hand toward the opponent's head. His right hand redirects the attacker's incoming left arm, down and away to the right side. (2) The opponent blocks the defender's left-hand strike and starts to throw a forward kick. Seeing the initiation of the kick, the defender steps to the right with his right leg while throwing his left foot forward to the side of the incoming kick. He seamlessly retracts his leg to catch the attacker's heel with his own, pulling him off balance. (3) While stepping down with his left foot, the defender spins right 180 degrees with his whole body. His right foot lands closer to the opponent, while his left foot rotates on the heel and his right elbow strikes the opponent's chin, which breaks the opponent's neck—a *coup de grâce*.

Within every movement in this sequence, the master perceives even more than those with less experience and skill. He knows which muscles are appropriately used and which are not. He recognizes the potential for many alternate applications within each movement. He visualizes the body's internal structure, including its skeletal alignment, the integrity of each joint, and where hindrances may appear in the respiratory, nervous, and circulatory systems. Beyond this, the master senses the movement of internal energies (*qi*) as they flow through the meridians. He identifies strengths and weaknesses, and how the sources of power are tapped in the overall body mechanics. Finally, he recognizes that the entire martial routine has been guided by the mind. Even the attacker's state of mind can be intuited.

I think of my master. He saw so much more than I.

A Monitoring Touch

Whenever two people meet in a confrontation, the most common point of contact is the crossing of forearms. This happens if one reaches or strikes toward the other, and the aggressive move is met with a block or deflection. Sidestepping such attacks makes it easy to avoid the danger, but then you may feel apprehension for a subsequent attack of some sort. After avoiding the first attack by the block or deflection, it is common to immediately pull the arm back into a guard stance. However, if you remove the arm from contact, you may be missing an opportunity.

Some masters prefer to initiate or to maintain light contact with an opponent as soon as their forearms meet. The contact itself is safe, so if there is no reason to break it, the touch can be used to sense the attacker's next move. From the point of contact, it is possible to feel where the attacker is moving next, no matter which direction.

If you have made contact with your right arm against an attacker's right arm, he may next attempt to strike with his left hand. As his left arm starts to move forward, it is possible to feel the backward movement in his right arm. As one shoulder moves, the other shoulder must also move, and you will get an early indicator of what is coming. Because of the swiveling connection between the shoulders and arms, you can manipulate the forward arm to prevent being struck. For example, if after defending with the right forearm against a right punch, the attacker attempts to strike with his left hand, you can catch and move the attacker's right arm to control the left arm. The control of one arm affects the movement of the other.

A forward movement will increase pressure against the arm. A retreat will lessen the pressure. Shifting left or right, sinking or rising, all can be sensed in the arm contact. In these cases it is important to use a light sticking energy [*ting jin*] so as not to lose contact. This way you can continue to monitor the attacker's intentions. Maintain contact and follow the opponent to sense his full body movement.

Humans are made of muscle and bone, and a tense musculature is most conducive to transmitting movement through the body. Moving one part immediately causes the other parts to move. The more relaxed the body, the more difficult it is to sense its movements at the forearm. This is another reason highly skilled masters favor relaxation in their styles. As the masters state: "With the simple light touch, you can know your opponent, while he will not be able to know you."

The above paragraphs discuss the method of monitoring the movements and intentions of an attacker utilizing a sensing forearm. We can also use the same method by making contact with the legs. While using the forearm or leg in this way, you must also be aware of potential dangers to these limbs. If the arms and torso stay relaxed, they can easily move to prevent any advantage for the opponent, such as being grabbed or locked. Keeping the legs safe is more difficult because even masters are often not relaxed enough in the legs to be mobile at all times.

One Technique, Multiple Applications

The numerous fighting styles preserve much of their systems in codified routines. As students begin to learn any routine, they stand at the doorway to the art. The first step through the threshold is to begin to memorize each individual movement, one by one. It helps to learn an application for each movement and visualize it during practice. Then each movement can be retained and become habit. At this point, the student becomes free from the work of memorization and can actually practice the routine to improve it.

Often, beginning students think there is one application for each movement, while actually there are many variations. It is certainly beneficial to learn the routine with one technique in mind for each movement, which provides a standard form. As students get more familiar with each movement, it becomes easier to gradually add variations that fit their advancing skill level. The form develops the fundamentals of the fighting system. An infinite number of applications can be built from this solid base.

A technique common to all systems is a ward-off with the palm facing upward. It can be used against a punch to the head. Some, because they keep firm in their stance, must block with great strength to knock away the oncoming arm and prevent being struck. If the attacker strikes with his left hand and you step to your left side, the ward-off can be done without tension, since both the shift and ward-off are working in tandem. If you sink low to evade the attacker's punch, a block may not be necessary at all, and the arm can be used to throw a strike instead. Alternatively, you can step behind the attacker's lead leg and use the same arm to throw the attacker over your well-positioned leg.

These examples of the basic ward-off show how the arm movement can be used to block, deflect, strike, or throw. More applications are possible. Analyze the practice routines, and many variations can be discovered for each individual movement. When under close scrutiny, some variations quickly present themselves. However, a good number of variations will remain invisible to all except the gifted masters. One example is provided next.

An approaching attacker may place both his hands on your forearms. If he pushes on one arm, you can turn to deflect the push. The attacker may immediately try to push with his other arm, and you can deflect it the same way. You don't force the pushes away. Your relaxed arms follow his turning waist, giving the attacker nothing to push against. This same body movement can be utilized when the attacker comes from the back. If he grabs you from behind, around the shoulders, you can move quickly left then right, letting your elbows strike his lower rib cage toward the kidneys. Same technique, but applied in a totally different direction.

Over a long period of investigating the potential uses for each technique, the multiplication produces an amazing number of applications for the martial art repertoire. The number of possible techniques is enhanced by principles that allow a smooth transition between techniques. These principles include relaxation, body alignment, and focus. Without these essentials, the number of techniques and applications is not so meaningful as one would expect, since the practitioner will not be able to effortlessly employ them with power and accuracy.

Bellows Breathing

When to inhale and exhale while practicing routines or techniques? This question echoes constantly among practitioners. Methods abound, and they can choose which one they believe may best suit their needs. Many ways of breathing are found in martial and nonmartial traditions. There is a strong influence from the Indian yogic practices that have also blended with Daoist longevity techniques.

Inhale when arms go outward and exhale
when arms return close to the body.
Or, breathe in the opposite manner.

Hold the breath for a quick pause in between
the inhalation and exhalation. The pause can be
for a split second, or until your face turns blue.

Breathe in through the nose and exhale through the mouth. Or, do this in the opposite manner.

While exhaling, expand the abdomen.
While inhaling, let the abdomen contract.

Tense the torso, shoulders, arms, and hands while striking and exhaling. Or not.

The above give some indications of what can be involved when combining breathing methods with the fighting arts. These practices can become even more complex when other requirements are added, such as timing with specific physical postures and gestures, and internal visualizations.

All such breathing methods require the practitioner to constantly think of what is being done, when, and for how long. This may be fine for stationary sitting or standing practices, but for martial arts, we cannot allow streaming thoughts to impede the mind. They only interfere with combative movement. Daoist masters, who have a plethora of breathing techniques in their ancient tradition, favor a much simpler solution to martial practices: they use a bellows for an analogy.

A bellows is used to help start and keep fires burning. It is an essential instrument used in a forge. Open the handles of a bellows, and air is drawn inside it. Squeeze the handles together, and air is forced out. The bellows does not need to be prompted when to take air in or force it out. The movements of the handles make it happen spontaneously. So too with martial movement. If one executes any technique or routine with a relaxed body, the movements will cause the lungs to inhale and exhale. If there are tensions in the body, one's breath will become obstructed and irregular, bringing fatigue. Because the common person carries tensions, perhaps it is necessary to incorporate some breathing discipline into martial practice. For the masters, breathing is another skill brought into harmony with fighting skills.

Most martial art practitioners not only tense when in combat, but even when they are not in combat. There are many reasons for this. A major reason is that tensing the body gives a feeling of strength and power. As a major factor with the fighting arts, fear also figures in. It causes stress, which in turn gives rise to tension. However, practitioners with high-level skills exhibit fewer tensions in their techniques. Time and experience have taught them that the more relaxed they are while executing techniques, the more speed, fluidity, and power result. Tension causes hesitation in response and slows movement. Over time, tensions cause stiffness and even chronic pain.

The teachers who cultivate relaxation in their practice look for signs where tension occurs in their students. The most obvious locations are the shoulders and hands. For beginning students, it isn't obvious at all. The teacher constantly reminds them to relax, let the shoulders drop, and allow their wrists and fingers to release any rigidity and take their natural shape. Some students tighten their jaws and grit their teeth. Relaxing the back and legs is even more difficult to achieve.

Such tensions in the body affect fighting techniques. Outward movements can be held back by taut muscles, weakening strikes and throws. Tightness limits the height of kicks too. In these cases, the muscles contract even when one is trying to extend an arm or leg. Further examination of martial techniques also shows muscles being forced to overextend. So we actually have two types of tension, the contracting and extending types of movements. Overextending by itself can cause damage. It is also very dangerous in combat, as the elbow joints and knees are targets that are easy to injure and break.

The body postures of leading masters—the standard-bearers of combat systems—are not governed by rigidity. Their forms are not compacted, nor are they overly enlarged. The goal is to be natural and move naturally. In order to rid the body of unnecessary tensions, most masters persistently try to (1) identify where tensions arise and (2) understand why they arise. Their vigilance brings greater awareness and opportunities to tame the tensions.

A regular routine for calming the body is to stand quietly and mentally scan yourself from head to toe:

(1) Relax any tensions in the head and forehead, and around the eyes, ears, and jaw. Even the inside of the head should feel like an expanding sponge, loosening any tightness.
(2) Move next to the neck and shoulders. Let them be as natural as possible, and feel the arms hanging loosely at the sides. The wrist joints and fingers are loose. An alignment from shoulders to fingertips will occur, guided by gravity.
(3) Let the breathing happen on its own, smooth and even. Let the abdomen be at ease.
(4) Notice how balance affects how much muscle is used to stand. The legs are weight bearing. While relaxing the legs, include the ankles and toes. Discover what tensions are used to stand, and learn what tensions are not necessary. Balance makes it all easier.
(5) Hold the position and mentally scan the body again to let any tightness melt away.
(6) Remember how the body feels during this exercise and let it be the reference for studying tensions present in martial movements.

No Resistance, No Pressure

There is power in pressure. This is the significance of the Chinese characters *ya* and *li*. The character *li* shows an arm, the ancient Chinese radical for strength. The etymology of the character *ya* explains it as something "full of dirt." Dirt is heavy and causes pressure. It can exert great force against whatever it comes upon. The amount of pressure is in proportion to the amount of dirt. The same physics apply in martial practice.

During solo practice, we can identify many areas where pressure occurs. We only need to question what causes pressure. Where does "dirt" start to be felt on or in the body? The most notable locations are in the joints. They have an inherent range of comfortable motion. When moved beyond this range, problems start. When pushed too far, damage is done and great pain results. However, even a "dusting" of pressure has an effect. For example, when one executes a forward push with one leg in front and the other behind, the back leg usually provides the power for the forward movement. If the leg positioning is not in the most conducive alignment for the push, there results in some light friction in the knee. If the arms are not in the optimal position, stress can occur in the shoulders, elbows, and wrists. Often the pressure is so slight that it goes unnoticed. The amount of pressure varies according to how much the alignment is off. Better alignment makes for better movement.

The amount of pressure placed in the body during solo practice is relatively light, since you can control your own movements. However, when facing an opponent, the chances for pressure to occur are predictably much higher. The joints come under greater stress in competitive bouts. Grappling movements are designed to apply force against bone, such as the extended arm, for throws. Locks are effective because they place an opponent in compromised positions with pressure against joints and bones. An application with slightly more pressure or speed can easily turn a lock into a break.

A close look at body movement will show that an attacker's aggressive moves cause pressure in the body of the defender. By reacting, the defender usually creates additional pressures within his own body. Pressures resulting from pushing, pulling, and twisting play havoc on the joints, ligaments, muscles, and tendons. In fighting situations, this ends with injuries. For a solo physical exercise, the pressures can also cause damage. Too often a small, seemingly insignificant fault in movement, done repetitively over time, brings on physical problems.

It is also common to resist when pulled, as when an attacker grabs one's wrist. Moving in the direction of the pull makes it possible to maintain neutrality, and the elbow and shoulder joints will not be injured. So, when either pushed or pulled, resistance is the frequent response, a reaction associated with stress and potential injuries.

Whenever practicing a martial art, an important guideline is to not let pressure build in the body. This is possible only when there is no resistance. Pushing against a push—force against force—builds great pressure. By moving away from the push, or simply deflecting it to the side, you can stay relaxed and neutral. When practicing a martial art for combat or for health, it is certainly best to keep the body stress-free. Constant observation of how and when pressures arise during practice gives opportunities to make adjustments that can make movements safer and more efficient. This, in turn, proffers ways to improve fighting techniques.

Right, Wrong, or Variation

We have the Great Qing Legal Code, which contains 1,907 statutes. These serve as guidelines in determining right from wrong in particular cases, so proper penalties can be determined. Luckily, if one makes an erroneous movement in martial practice, a punishment by the heavy bamboo is not prescribed. However, students do pay a price for any mistakes made, great or small.

Sometimes a movement is executed so incorrectly that immediate injury results. The movement is easily judged as wrongly done. The results are the proof. However, in the vast majority of cases, the line distinguishing right from wrong is not so clear. An example is easily shown in the basic bow stance, standing as if ready to shoot an arrow. If ten students take this position, their toes will generally be angled in line with the shoulders and hips. The body parts are in perfect alignment. Then there is an exception: one student's back foot angles farther to the back. Both feet are pointing in different directions. Is this stance incorrect? There is a clear difference in his stance versus his teacher's.

Judging by the standard is not always logical. Have the same ten students face forward, standing in a relaxed stance with both feet close together. Most toes will be pointing straight ahead. With some, however, their toes may be pointing slightly outward, feet in a more triangular alignment. Perhaps some will be pigeon-toed. If the teacher tells them to make their feet straight, these students will probably feel pressures in their knees or ankles. The wider the angle, the more tension is required to force the feet to point straight ahead.

Upon close scrutiny, it becomes clear that all students have their own natural alignment, which needs to be taken under consideration before any judgment can be made. The standard for making a judgment is not solely the template provided by the master's postures and movements, but the ideal for which each individual can move best according to his or her own innate physical being.

An experienced master can recognize variations among students' postures and movements due to what may be faults in comprehending and executing techniques. At the same time, the master should distinguish such faults from variations due to physical constitution. Instruction guides students toward perfection in movement according to their own unique attributes. In the end, the student must discover what is most natural for him- or herself, taking into account such internal structures as the skeletal and muscular systems. A good martial artist should not struggle through movements. When the art is mastered, techniques feel effortless.

Another area of contention involves the practical functions of techniques as incorporated into practice routines. A few examples will be useful. (1) *Wave hands like clouds*: Some say the fingers should point upward at the top of the circles, while others say they should be horizontal. (2) *Monkey retreats*: While stepping in retreat, one hand pushes forward and the other arm moves backward at head level, or curves downward and back past the hip.

In the first example, a student will learn one method from his teacher and therefore think the other method is incorrect. In actuality, the one method focuses on the hand and the other on the forearm. They are slightly different applications and both correct for the differing situations. In the second example, if an attacker strikes high, the defender can deflect the incoming arm while pushing forward. If the attacker strikes low toward the stomach, then the defender drops his arm to the side. Again, this illustrates two different responses to two different attacks. Both are correct for the situations.

Whenever judging applications, it is necessary to see the many possible variations. If the movement fits the situation, it is correct. Then what makes a movement wrong? Certainly if the movement doesn't fit the situation. Blocking high when an attack is low is fruitless. The question of right or wrong has much to do with the quality of movement and embodying combat principles. For example, a student tries a two-hand forward push but is not very successful. Perhaps the arms were not in proper alignment with the legs or torso? Perhaps the elbows were held outward, away from the body, and thus also not in alignment with the legs? That is the right application done wrong.

The principles of application are the real guidelines. We judge the body movement and applications by the theories adopted and utilized by the masters. These theories contain differences according to experience and insight. If the theory is incorrect, then the practice will be incorrect. Some use right methods in the wrong way. Some use faulty methods with success. A duty for every martial artist is not only to practice physical techniques, but to investigate combat theory. In this way, differences between right and wrong become clearer, and gray areas remain under question.

In large part, martial artists gain respect and admiration for their abilities to demonstrate extraordinary feats of fighting skills. Those watching are amazed by high jumps that defy gravity, leg splits done with ease, and strikes flashing like lightning. But such remarkable muscular exhibitions, feats of balance, twists, and rolls are not the main qualities the true masters find most worthy. Here is why.

A highly dedicated fighter spends hours in daily practice, stretching leg muscles to gain flexibility. Over months and years, his legs become strong and can keep stability in extremely low postures. No others can sink so low into an outspread position. Truly impressive, but trying to move from this width is nearly impossible. The stance is difficult to achieve, so difficult that it proves useless for any practical martial art. Being stretched out so wide, there is not enough spring in either leg to move to one side or the other. Overly strenuous movements bring a struggle within the body and way too often lead to damaging oneself, pulling muscles, breaking ligaments, cracking bone and cartilage.

The great masters I've met are not impressed by the excessive, theatrical, or acrobatic. The real purpose of martial arts is not for show, and they are not gymnastic exercises. The masters particularly deride displays of ego by proud peacocks. A high level of difficulty for any movement or technique does not mean it is practical for self-defense. Fancy movements often grab attention while distracting from the principles that are more conducive for effective fighting. Any serious martial artist is cautious in practice, training and nurturing the body to be healthy and fluent in fighting techniques.

A desire to become superhuman and to show others the rare levels of difficulty possible in human movement can lead one astray from the guiding principles of the martial arts: seek to move in the most efficient way possible, without damaging oneself from the faulty ways of training.

Mirrorlike Mind

Before the introduction of Western glass mirrors during the Ming Dynasty [1368–1644], exquisite bronze mirrors were common here for over a thousand years. Most were handheld circular disks made of cast bronze, highly polished on one side and decorated on the reverse. Besides the obvious use, Daoists would set them on the ground to collect morning dew for making elixirs. Some wore them on their backs to ward off mountain demons. When bright light hit the polished side of a magic mirror, it reflected designs from the reverse side, projecting them on a wall.

Philosophers have used the mirror as a symbol for the mind. Humans are susceptible to many sorts of mental disruptions, especially from fluctuating emotions. This "worldly dust" prevents the mirror from reflecting properly. In the *Daodejing,* Laozi asks: "Can you polish your mysterious mirror and leave no blemish?" This polishing method entails calming the emotions so the mind clearly reflects reality as it truly exists. Like a calm pond without a single wave, the water can reflect geese flying overhead, the image displayed without distortion. The water does not hold on to the images but lets them go by.

Excited by anger, fear, or hate, a swordsman's movements will be affected, causing hurried attacks and awkward defense. Therefore, the mental state is of utmost importance for the martial artist. The polished mind reflects the reality of any combative confrontation. Seeing without emotional dust to cloud the vision, one can defend oneself effortlessly and without worry. The attainment of a mirrorlike mind has been the ultimate goal for many philosophical and religious traditions. It finds application in the martial traditions as well.

The Martial Family

Life in China is guided by the "three teachings, harmonious as one": Confucianism, Daoism, and Buddhism. These great traditions color every aspect of our existence. Many concepts are held in common, but those that hold our fabric of society together are largely derived from the great sage Confucius. Some of the more important Confucian virtues deal with respect for parents and elders, loyalty, kindness, affection, trustworthiness, honesty, and harmony. Those who do not put these virtues into daily practice should be ashamed, as their behaviors bring disruption to society and dishonor to the family.

Confucius saw the family as the key to social order. His wisdom is praised for the practical aspects that secure peace and harmony. Deeply embedded in this philosophy is a profound respect for elders and teachers. Their wisdom is derived from great years of experience. The term *laoshi* does not simply mean "teacher." *Lao* means old, and *shi* indicates a teacher. One needs years of experience to gain knowledge.

Some disagree with the Confucian family concept, such as the relationship between husband and wife. They may say, "A teapot has one spout, but many cups." However, a husband with more than one wife or lover will fail to properly attend to the family. We have the character *jian*, which is composed of three women. It carries the meanings of adultery, rape, treason, and malevolence. On the other hand, the character for peace is *an*—one woman under a roof—meaning safe, secure, and quiet.

The social structure of the Chinese family was duplicated in the martial family. There is an organized hierarchy under the master, followed by senior to junior students. The students' responsibilities include loyalty and respect to their teacher, and kindness and affection to fellow students. All students are dedicated to their teacher, and only one teacher. If a student reaches a high skill level, the teacher may give permission for him or her to study with another master; otherwise, it is like a husband asking his wife if it is okay to spend one night a week with another woman and expecting no repercussions. Even asking for permission is offensive and shows a lack of respect and appreciation.

Why should a master teach a student higher-level skills when the student is not dedicated to the martial family? A precautionary practice has been adopted within martial and medical families to safeguard the higher teachings. Whenever knowledge can be used by the unscrupulous, responsible people must guard it. This is especially true with the potentially lethal arts. High-level martial teachings are preserved by a ring of secrecy, reinforced by social responsibilities outlined in Confucian principles.

The stable order provided by Confucian ideals allows a martial family to preserve and enhance the art over generations. It is common for a master to pass on all his or her knowledge to three of the most-deserving students. The honored students are not selected solely on their physical abilities, but more importantly on the uprightness of their character.

Daoist Philosophy

Over the centuries, some individuals realized the value of applying Daoist theory to their martial practice. I've been mesmerized by a few rare masters who have been able to employ the subtle ideas into their arts, enhancing their power, speed, and fluidity in movement. However, the vast majority of masters—regardless of time and effort expended—fail to bring these Daoist principles to life. It's worth taking a brief look at the history and the essential concepts of this philosophical school.

The roots certainly come from the *Book of Changes* [*Yijing*], a divination manual from the Western Zhou period (1000–750 BCE), probably based on much earlier methods seeking to commune with the supernatural. During the Warring States period (475–221 BCE) and later, the *Changes* became a guide for understanding the cosmos with insightful philosophical commentaries. These rich sources of thought gave a foundation to the Confucian and Daoist traditions. Both Laozi and Zhuangzi, the authors of the *Daodejing* and the *Zhuangzi* respectively, were inspired by the brilliant primeval perceptions. They presented the key Daoist concepts, which we can look at here as they relate to combatives.

Ten Thousand Things

All that exists between heaven and earth is often referred to as *ten thousand things*, which is a blanket term meaning the innumerable. Things, infinitely numerous in shapes and sizes, dazzle our senses with an ever-changing kaleidoscope of colors, sounds, aromas, tastes, and textures. From birth, we are forced to find our place within this ever-churning world. The philosophy we develop can provide the insights and skills that determine how successful we will be. This is our means for survival.

During the formation of early Chinese culture, philosophers recognized that, in order to solve any complex problem, it would be easier if the ten thousand things surrounding a given matter could be simplified. What is the most important aspect of the problem? What roles do other factors play, and which are really significant? Through such questioning, early philosophers were actually developing a highly sophisticated mode of reasoning. They found it useful to categorize the ten thousand things to better adapt to their environment.

A parallel can be found in martial art practice, in which the student is initially overwhelmed by ten thousand movements. Here the student is challenged to find a way to properly master the complexity of all the movements—as well as find a self-defense strategy for facing multiple attackers. A step along this path involves the discovery of categories by which the combat movements can be better understood and performed.

The Ways and Means of Five Forces

Stopping to contemplate the world, philosophers gave attention to the ten thousand things that appeared between heaven and earth. They looked closely in every direction. As a person peers outward, he realizes he himself forms the center of his existence, the center of the universe. Likewise, a martial artist can find himself at the center of combat, flanked by opponents.

Perhaps this orientation between man and his universe led the Chinese to the idea of *wuxing*. An analysis of the characters *wu* and *xing* helps us clarify the general meaning usually given to the compound term as *five forces* or *five phases*. Wu simply stands for the number five. In ancient times, it was written like an *X*, where four lines indicated the directions from a common central focus. Later, a line was placed above and another below the *X*, symbolic of heaven and earth. This is similar to man's position on earth. Only from his own viewpoint can he look out into all directions under heaven.

Xing carries with it such meanings as to *go, operate, conduct*, or *set into motion*. Combined with wu, we have five active forces, or movers. They represent five basic phases through which matter continuously transforms itself, abstract forces that keep the ten thousand things in operation.

Besides being associated with the five spatial directions (north, south, east, west, and center), the wuxing concept was suitably applied to other aspects of nature. A partial list indicates its significance as a comprehensive tool for understanding the ten thousand things. In particular, it often was associated with the seasons, animals, weather, bodily organs, numbers, musical notes, colors, and even flavors.

How do the five forces work? According to Daoist expositions, they seem to work quite easily in their interactions. Just as one season naturally follows another, any one phase is connected to the next. Plus, all phases are interrelated in some way, each having its own characteristics and influences. In short, each plays its part in an overall process of construction and destruction that keeps the ten thousand things in movement. Due to cause and effect, they flow in cycles, passing from one phase to the next until completing a circuit. By an intimate understanding of the laws involved in such changes, man can better adapt himself to continual flux in the world.

The theory of five forces was applied to all fields of study, including astronomy, divination, medicine, agriculture, politics, art, religion, and martial arts. It served as a valuable schematic upon which subjects could be analyzed and understood within their specialized sphere of changing relationships. Thus, within their changes, an underlying order and permanence could still be found.

China's ancient philosophers were seeking a practical way to obtain the insight and skills necessary to master life. Although wuxing theory proved very useful, its application was actually still so complex that only the most gifted of sages could successfully employ it to advantage. Driven by emotions, most humans become easily distracted, entangled, and confused by five ever-changing variables. Laozi was clearly aware of this, writing

> The five primary colors blind the eyes.
> The five flavors confuse one's sense of taste.
> The five tones bring on a loss of hearing.
> Therefore, in a sagely government: He is for
> the essence and discards the superficial.
> Thus he remains undistracted and focused.

The wuxing were understood to be the simplified basis of the ten thousand things. In order to be more workable, would it be possible to simplify further? Chinese sages did just that by implementing the duality of yin and yang. In a similar manner, the martial artist eventually finds order within the complexity of movements comprising fighting techniques. Some practitioners become infatuated with many techniques in their routines. They do not heed Laozi's advice, and instead they get lost in ten thousand movements. If a routine is categorized into sections and sequences become familiar, the routine is performed with less difficulty. As a result, the practitioner feels as if he is moving through sections of the routine rather than many individual movements.

The Bi-ways of Yin and Yang

We walk a road on two feet and view the world through only two eyes. In the fourth century BCE, the Chinese also formulated a polar view of the world with the theory of yin-yang. By the Han Dynasty (202 BCE–220 CE), this yin-yang school absorbed that of wuxing. Together they offered a comprehensive system useful not only for analysis, but also in the control and manipulation of all areas to which they were applied.

There are earthy roots to the yin-yang theory. Sinologists believe that the ancient characters were derived in part as symbolic images of the daily fluctuation between day and night, or more precisely, light and dark. The yang character shows the sun on the horizon, radiating its brilliance down on the earth. As a result, yang came to imply a varied list of sunlike attributes, such as heat, day, clarity, brightness, and fire. Yin is composed of *jin*, a phonetic meaning "now" and *yun* meaning "cloudy." Therefore, yin became associated with cloudlike characteristics, including cold, night, shade, darkness, and water. Oddly enough, no written character can fully express the meaning with which yin-yang became associated. Because the symbolism of language failed to convey the meaning of yin-yang, a more appropriate symbol was required. Of all of the cosmological diagrams invented in China, the taiji symbol is no doubt the most famous. It also remains the most useful symbol for expressing the yin-yang theory. The characters for taiji should first be analyzed before discussing the symbol itself.

When the characters for *taiji* are broken down, the individual character *tai* we find refers to something "very big" or "extreme." It resembles a stick figure stretching his limbs out to their limits in four directions. *Ji* is more complicated. It also has a significance of "extreme," but more importantly a "pole," the extreme of any axis. In ancient times, *ji* was a common word for the "ridgepole" upon which the structure of a house would rest. With reference to cosmology, taiji is the "supreme ultimate principle," the cosmological ridgepole that supports the whole universe.

In philosophical terms, taiji is the absolute. It is the most basic principle upon which the ten thousand things rest. An absolute is so limitless and pervasive that it does not have any visible signs to be perceived. For this reason, yin-yang became its first visible attributes. The symbol for taiji, or the supreme ultimate, is the intertwining of yin and yang. The parts are not static, but are constantly in movement, varying their relationship in fluctuating percentages or even transforming one into the other. Through the varied interactions of yin-yang, the universe is kept in motion. No aspect of creation exists without their signature. Laozi wrote

> The ten thousand things keep yin on their
> backs and embrace yang in their arms.
> Through the appropriate mixing of these
> energies, they arrive at a state of harmony.

The yin-yang interplay is the foundation of boxing routines. It is the impetus of the flowing movements. Throughout the routines, practitioners experience the fluctuating pulse of yin and yang.

In Daoism, wuxing and yin-yang serve to categorize the ten thousand things. This helps one to understand the universe in its varied aspects. Wuxing and yin-yang also demonstrate how the universe operates. Boxers likewise illustrate the flow of movement through positional phases and fluctuations between yin and yang. On an even subtler level, movement is brought about from stillness. Stillness is found in the Dao.

Heavenly Identity: The High-Way of Daoism

The *Daodejing* states:

> Even before Heaven and Earth, something emerged
> from primordial chaos. It is profoundly silent,
> tranquil, and unpolluted! It is self-contained

and unwavering. We can regard it the mother of Heaven and Earth. Since it is nameless, we simply refer to it as the "Way" (Dao).

The Dao holds the power to reconcile opposites. We find this in the highest levels of martial practice. It is made known when the practitioner transcends the complexity of the ten thousand movements, the arbitrary groupings of sequential techniques, and even mind-body duality. This is a mystic state that does not limit itself to boxing.

A dominant thought existing in Laozi's time is found in the *Book of Odes*: "Heaven in producing mankind annexed its laws to every faculty and relationship. Man possessed of this nature should strive to develop his endowment to perfection." A heavenly identity, or Dao realization, comes to one through polishing the mirrorlike mind, cleansing away its mundane dust. Laozi further advised one to rid himself of desires in order to observe the Dao's secrets. Zhuangzi called this a process of "purifying the mind."

Dao realization is of great importance because whoever attains this state takes on all the attributes of the eternal Dao. Why this is important in martial arts can be discerned from a quote from the *Daodejing*: "If you're one with the Dao, to the end of your days you'll suffer no harm."

Laozi further states

He who knows how to live can travel abroad
without fearing the rhinoceros or tiger.
He can not be injured in battle for in him a
rhinoceros can find no place to thrust its horn,
a tiger can find no place to use its claws,
and a weapon has no place to pierce.
How is this possible? Because he who
is in harmony with the Dao has no place
for death to enter.

The Dao is described in Chinese literature as being complete and whole. As such, it is the abode of stillness and tranquility. It is the "mother of the ten thousand things." Laozi writes: "The Way [Dao] gives birth to them, nourishes them, matures them, completes them, rests them, rears them, supports them, and protects them." All these words inspire martial artists to embrace the Dao.

Living Daoism

A boxing student passes through various psychological stages in experiencing the complexity of combat routines and applications. It begins as a mysterious hodgepodge of techniques. In time, the numerous movements within the routines become easier to understand and perform, as regular practice brings familiarity with the sets. The wuxing and yin-yang concepts help us understand the underlying process of change within the routines. We also learn the inherent relationship that exists within the unity of all body parts as utilized in the movements.

At the highest level of practice, the completeness and wholeness of the boxing routines find a parallel in the oneness of Dao. When we transcend the dualism of mind and body, the boxing routines seem to flow of their own accord, as natural as a flowing river. This is fighting in the state of "nondoing" (*wuwei*). A solo performance in this state is characterized by tranquility and freedom from thought, which for the martial artist has other implications as well. It makes the power (*de*) of Dao available, for in self-defense it is necessary to move spontaneously with the accuracy and strength possible only through the complete unification of human thought and movement.

What we have analyzed is the discovery of Daoist principles in martial routines. Here, the inner workings of the individual are found, presenting the physical and mental operations as they are seen in the solo routines. There are also other practices, such as push-hands and paired forms. These practices seek to let the individual discover his relationship with others.

Usually, those who have provided commentaries about Daoist philosophy start with the Dao, move to yin-yang, then the five phases, and lastly the ten thousand things. However, another major theme in Daoist thought is the necessity to return to the source, or return to the mother. This little essay therefore starts with our place surrounded in the reality of ten thousand things, and then it looks to the path of return. We are but companions on the Way.

Daoist Quest for Immortality

Zhuangzi wrote of longevity exercises. Qin Shi Huang (d. 210 BCE), our first emperor, patronized Daoist alchemists to make elixirs for prolonging life. Since those ancient days, the undaunted quest for immortality continues with fervor. Zhang Daoling created the Daoist movement called the Celestial Masters after Laozi appeared to him in 142 CE. Over the centuries, the Celestial Masters sect grew, spread, and is strong today. This group and others are responsible for the dispersion of Daoist practices throughout China.

When Buddhism gained ground in China, Daoism faded some. As a result, Daoism copied certain organizational aspects from the Buddhists, establishing a hierarchy, building temples, and competing in debates under emperors and political leaders. Various Daoist schools evolved, but the basic principles remained as a common denominator. However, some branches, as those expounding secret sexual practices for strengthening qi, were highly criticized. In contrast, the Celestial Masters included 180 precepts on morality, believing that any sinful act is contrary to the Daoist Way and damages the individual's mind, body, and spirit.

Ge Hong (283–343 CE), "the Master Who Embraces Simplicity," wrote his text allowing us to learn of longevity techniques and make elixirs. Many use his methods, while others have their own regimens and varied combinations of practices: creating and swallowing golden saliva, breathing like a tortoise, stretching like a tiger, excluding grains from the diet, digesting elixirs including cinnabar, rubbing and tapping vital points, massaging the organs, chanting sacred sounds, and visualizing qi moving through orbits within the body.

Today we find a stunning variety of Daoist health practices geared to longevity and immortality. Earlier efforts usually involved something that could be ingested, and so are associated with external alchemy [*waidan*]. The time, money, and effort devoted to these practices had few results, with negligible lengthening of lifespan, and a good number of devotees died from ingesting poisons. More have since turned to internal alchemy [*neidan*], special physical, mental, and spiritual practices designed with the same original goals as external alchemy.

Rather than using a cauldron to make elixirs, the internal school uses the human body itself as the vessel for cultivating the three treasures [*jing*, essence; *qi*, energy; and *shen*, spirit]. Many benefits result by nourishing these treasures. Some methods focus on the mind, such as Daoist yoga, and meditative and visualization practices done sitting or lying down. Other methods call for mind-body work, as we find in the many systems of *daoyin* [stretching and pulling] and *qigong* [exercising vital energy].

Some exercises focus on maintaining and nourishing health, while others are practiced for spiritual development, or to bring extraordinary strength to the body, particularly for martial purposes. Although created by a military general, Yue Fei, the Eight Pieces of Brocade exercises are an example of medical qigong. Bodhidharma's Muscle-Tendon Changes usually utilizes eighteen exercises for specific bodily areas and energy meridians. The Six Healing Sounds may be the result of adding twenty-four movements to an earlier system of vocal exercises. The sounds made include a hiss, yawn, sigh, puff, and laugh. Each is pronounced in the first tone [the high, level tone of the four basic tones in Mandarin], and all are believed to affect the health of the heart, spleen, pancreas, lungs, kidneys, and the triple burners [three areas identified in traditional Chinese medicine in the upper, middle, and lower parts of the body]. Created by the famed physician Hua Tuo (c. 140–208 CE), the Five Animal Frolics consist of deep stretching and breathing based on the movements of the tiger, deer, bear, monkey, and bird. To some degree these help in rehabilitation, but they are primarily practiced to nourish health and prevent disease and common problems associated with aging.

There are a number of branches to the systems noted above, plus other similar types of exercises. They find a common thread in their purpose of maintaining and improving physical, mental, and spiritual conditions. For true Daoists, the ultimate goal is to achieve unity of the Dao through such practices. Each of these methods has something useful for martial art practitioners: the medical knowledge helps keep the body in good condition, stretching ensures flexibility, meditation calms the mind, and the diet nourishes, thus creating a philosophy that fuses into a martial system as embodied in the individual.

Since there are innumerable Daoist practices associated with health and longevity, there is certainly a big variety of theories and practices that individuals can funnel into their martial practice. I've met high-level practitioners in major Daoist centers, such as the White Cloud Monastery here in Beijing, and others in mountain seclusion—hermits cultivating the Dao in harmony within natural surroundings. The pristine air and tranquility of the uplands are especially conducive to Daoist disciplines. No doubt this is why the character for "immortal" (仙) is composed of the characters for a person (人) and mountain (山).

A word of caution to those pursuing the martial and Daoist paths: the Dao lets us play tricks on ourselves! There is resolve to the paradox that the path is easy but difficult to set foot on. Those who have not yet embodied the Dao can certainly be swayed from the path by human foibles, drawn off track by misguided fantasies or faith in untested theories. An alchemist dies by his own poison. A fighter is defeated by one with more insight into the art. It takes great patience to let the Dao reveal itself. It can't be forced. Enjoy the slow unveiling and, perhaps one day, you too can join the ranks of Immortal Swordsman Lu Dongbin.

Finding a Master, Finding a Disciple

Master: one who possesses great skill or proficiency, an expert with the most complete knowledge in an art. What are the requirements for a martial artist to be honored with the title of master? We have to admit that it is a relative term and takes meaning only when used in comparison with others. So, we use an imaginary grading system, ranking practitioners from novice to grandmaster. We visualize a ranking scale according to those martial artists we have come to know over the years, from the novice to the most exemplary.

In Beijing, new masters regularly move here from all over the country. As a result, at times our scale for judging the top master needs to be extended beyond the present scale. So, we recalibrate. Even the word scale means "to climb." A new exemplar becomes our model of aspiration. Whatever scale we presently hold in mind can therefore change. But this is Beijing, the capital of the Middle Kingdom. In a hundred years since the end of the preceding Ming Dynasty [1644], the great Qing has doubled the population to nearly 180 million. There are many more masters, but rarely does one replace the presently recognized grandmaster.

In the smaller cities and villages, the master with the highest skill level is often not so high. He is only the best among known practitioners in the area, and he bears the standard of the local combat system. Oddly enough, if we travel to areas so remote that even small villages do not exist, we can find great masters, recluses living in high mountain grottos. On extremely rare occurrences, we may have the fortune to encounter a master who possesses such wonderful skills that we need to recalibrate and redefine the word "master," giving a whole new meaning to the title. Such encounters usually require proper introductions and a period to gain trust. A reputation may lead us to someone who may be a real master. Whether one is an impostor or a true master will be revealed by actions showing either low-level fighting skill or abilities way beyond the norm.

The Buddha said: "When the student is ready, the master will appear." This is not necessarily so. He who is judged as master on one scale may actually prove to be mediocre on another scale. In reality, it is very difficult to find a true master. A rare unicorn indeed. But whoever we meet who shares knowledge deserves love and respect as a teacher. With their instruction we are able to move another rung up the ladder, and we can humbly acknowledge the gifts we receive.

The great masters are laoshi, which defines them as experienced elders. Most cannot read or write. Most are unfamiliar with the great literature of medicine and philosophy, yet they show genius and perception way beyond the norm. Above all, they are virtuosos in their arts. Those possessing the most illustrious of skills and insights are dragons, and we may never have the blessing of bowing in their presence.

Now we come to the question: who should those true masters teach or not teach? According to Confucianism, the teacher-disciple relationship is one of the most valued. It is an extension of the father-son relationship, and the expected virtues for a disciple are the same as those for offspring, such as gratitude, respect, obedience, responsibility, and sincerity. The main bond here is the potentially lethal skills and knowledge of the martial arts. The skills taught can make a difference in whether or not one survives in a violent situation that could arise during any conflict, such as robbery, war, or personal disputes. The heavy weight of responsibility calls for strong moral character based on clear understanding of what is right and wrong, which guides when one should use deadly martial skills.

It is expected that a young novice would not be aware of the full significance of a martial tradition; however, it is also expected that the new student be of good character, as a reflection of his or her parents. For this reason, it is customary that someone familiar, someone the teacher respects, should introduce and vouch for the character of the new student. Without such a formal presentation, the teacher does not consider any new student. It is also the custom for the master to observe the student for at least three years for any character faults before teaching beyond the basics.

In order to learn any martial art, the student needs to be in good physical condition and maintain a healthy lifestyle. Learning combat skills takes much time and effort [*gongfu*], with persistent and consistent practice. In order to do this, the student's love of learning requires a mature attitude and stable emotions. In time, martial studies become intimately connected with all aspects of the student's life. The students who may possess these physical, mental, and moral qualities are rare. As a result, the master has as difficult a time in finding a worthy student as the student has in finding a true master. If fate allows the meeting of two such individuals, the student is expected to be a lifelong disciple, learning from the master, developing the martial system, and passing on the system to his future disciples.

Physical Connections

There's a Buddhist saying that goes something like this: "With the movement of a finger, the whole universe has changed." Thus are the connections of the universe. This serves as an analogy for the human body as well, and it plays great relevance for the martial artist.

Observe any combat technique being performed by someone new to martial art studies, and compare it to the way a master moves. Usually they are executed in very contrasting ways! The inexperienced direct their movements from the head and chest, leaning toward whatever direction they wish to go. They block, parry, and strike by moving the hands and arms with little waist or shoulder movement. The hands, elbows, head, knees, and feet are not coordinated. By contrast, experienced martial artists direct their movements from the lower dantian at the waist, the body's center of gravity. Defensive and offensive movements start at the waist and move through the shoulders to the arms and the hands. The whole body is coordinated in alignment with each movement.

The primary goal of the martial artist is to move in accord with the Dao. Actions follow the principle of wuwei: no action made is unnatural or in opposition to the way of nature. This theory sounds nice, but it is not easy to implement, so we rarely see it put fully into action. There seem to be too many body parts to manage properly, so any flaws large or small are revealed in the movements. Trying to individually coordinate all parts of the body in techniques is really impossible. However, there is a way to make it easier by focusing on one area that leads the other parts into a harmonious flow. The following illustration will provide insights.

Some artists have designed sculptures with hundreds of pieces connected by strings and hung by one point from a ceiling. When all pieces are lying on the ground, it is difficult to visualize what the sculpture should look like. If we pick up some pieces, it still gives no clue. But, when we lift up the lead piece to hang from the ceiling, all other pieces fall into place, revealing the full sculpture. For body mechanics, there is a similar principle with the main point being the waist. When the waist is moved, other parts of the body follow.

Another illustration will be helpful. If we take a long, narrow piece of cloth and start to turn it at the center, we'll notice a very important principle. As the center turns, it draws on all the threads in both directions toward the ends. The only time it does not immediately affect the ends is when there is slack in the cloth. Turn the center farther and eventually both ends will move. This is what occurs when the waist starts a movement.

The waist initiates a movement, which turns the shoulders, which in turn move the arms, elbows, and then the hands. High-level practitioners do this well. They have learned how to use the waist to move the upper part of the body in techniques, making them much more efficient and powerful than by moving the arms alone. However, an important factor often missed is how the waist also affects the lower body. As with the long piece of cloth, shouldn't a turning waist—the central part of the body—affect both the top and bottom? The waist initiates a movement, which turns the hips, which in turn move the thighs, knees, and then the feet.

For the lower body to be free enough to move under the direction of the waist, the leg muscles involved need to be relaxed enough to allow it. The legs provide the power and speed for movement. The waist gives direction. Three major obstacles tend to keep the lower body from following the waist: (1) the legs are weight bearing, (2) the defender fears an attacker, and (3) the defender has a limited idea of how strength is used in techniques. These can cause practitioners to keep the legs overly tense.

When the waist leads movement of the whole body, defensive and offensive techniques become much easier than when the limbs are stiff and moving independently. For example, if an attacker pushes against an arm, the defender should not focus on just the arm, but should immediately feel the push against his own center. This sets his waist in motion without any delay, allowing a counter to flow in defense. The opposite is true when touching an opponent's arm: one should feel the waist, the center of the opponent.

By implementing the above ideas into practice, the upper and lower body move together. The whole body can move as one, without tensions, without blockages, without hesitation.

The Body's Architectural Design

I often visit the Temple of Heaven and the Yonghe Lama

Temple here in Beijing. I've prayed in many others in distant areas, such as the Wannian Temple on Mount Emei in Sichuan Province and the White Horse Temple in Luoyang. These are truly inspirational spaces, especially when attended by the faithful who breathe life into the temples, much as the breath produces melodies from a flute. As wisps of fragrant incense carry prayers to the heavens, we can ponder the power of the gods as well as our own fragile earthly existence.

Our great temples inspire awe for their architectural designs. The architects have held a centuries-old secret that has kept their masterworks from destruction. This is the ability of the sacred structures to withstand tremendous forces from earthquakes that strike China's provinces. How can such large buildings and roofs made of heavy wooden beams withstand these shocks? By being reinforced with iron or wooden pegs and glue? Perhaps decorative bronze plates to add strength to the beams?

Close observation reveals the architects' secret. The heavy beams are not locked into place, but they utilize interlocking joints, intricate bracket sets [*dougong*] that help support the horizontal beams. These are not locked by fasteners or glue, but are free to move within extra space in the joints when earthquakes occur. The flexibility thus allows the temple's frame—its skeleton—to move during the impact from earthquakes, giving the building greater stability in movement. This architectural secret is also vital for the martial artist.

When a martial artist tries to remain firm, resisting any outside force, there is great chance for injury to occur because of the great pressures resulting from the confrontation. Even during solo practice, poor bodily alignment can cause great stresses. In addition to the physical stress, the actual implementation of combat techniques is also hindered, becoming less effective or perhaps not effective at all. Applying the secrets from temple architecture, we can improve our martial postures and transitional movements.

The first bodily system to examine is the skeletal system. The optimal ways of moving each joint need to be identified, as well as at what degree the movement starts to become impeded. A common mistake is to overextend the arms and legs, as when punching and kicking, which can easily damage the knee and elbow joints. Remember that the target of a strike is not at the end of the movement, or at the point of farthest extension.

For the skeletal system to function as nature designed it to move, we should give much attention to the muscular system. Muscle tensions push and pull the bones and joints, and therefore it is easy to force the skeleton out of its natural alignment. Muscles can tear. Tendons snap. Vertebrae slip. Nerves get pinched. In addition, even the inner organs and the five senses can be adversely affected.

For a martial artist, the body is a temple designed by nature to move effectively and efficiently when its general alignment is maintained. Whenever the laws of kinetics are abused, as in lower-level martial arts, the body will not function at its best, and injuries are likely to occur. The higher level of martial arts has developed in accord with the natural human body structure. Combat techniques can be done extremely well without bringing injury upon oneself, much like the sacred temple's ability to remain unscathed by the destructive powers of typhoons and earthquakes. The level of mastery reflects one's ability to move with the Dao.

Maintaining and Improving Health

Heavenly yang energy comingles with earthly yin energy, flowing through "dragon veins" between sky and land. Air and water circulate in a similar manner. However, when they are stagnant, they produce foul smells and form areas that breed sicknesses. On the human level, when the body's energy stagnates, illnesses arise. When the body's energy flows unhampered throughout the system, it nurtures the organs and keeps the body healthy. Proper martial art practice done regularly keeps the body's energy in motion, nourishing all aspects of health.

Most of our everyday activities involve physical movements that are habitually done and work only specific body parts. In some cases the repetition associated with certain jobs is harmful, affecting particular muscle groups and joints, for example. When a person focuses on one aspect of the fighting arts, say kicking, this can be damaging too. So, it is beneficial to practice a well-rounded art that involves the whole body. Of utmost importance here is not just what we practice, but how we practice. The exercise regimen should be balanced, safe, and in line with the principles of human kinetics. With the desire to become famous, many simply ruin their bodies beyond repair.

Many great teachers utilize stretching-pulling exercise [daoyin] to limber up the body. These exercises focus on slowly moving into postures that stretch the muscles to a comfortable extreme and loosen every joint and tendon. These are wonderful supplementary practices because combative techniques are safer when not done to such extremes, surely not when done with any speed. If martial-like movements are done for stretching-pulling, then they should be practiced slowly and in a very relaxed manner.

Martial movements are the core of our exercises. New students should start at a fairly slow tempo for some months and gradually increase the practice speed as the body moves better and better in a unified flow of action. The techniques are great in variety, working each muscle, ligament, and joint. As the mind focuses on each movement, the heart will beat in harmony with the actions. The lungs also function in accord with each movement. All these internal workings are conducive for calming the nervous system and mental faculty. Vital energy [qi] responds. Unhindered by muscular blockages and mental agitation, the energy streams to the organs and fosters the whole frame with strength.

The word of caution here is that even famous teachers sometimes recommend methods that are harmful to practitioners. They may be teaching styles that are impressive and more suitable for young practitioners, but may leave them somewhat broken as they age. It is more impressive to see centenarians practice who can still move as if they are teenagers. They can do so only if they have practiced wisely all their lives, careful to not injure their bodies, while nourishing them constantly. With proper practice, great benefits come and will remain into the twilight years, such as great balance, fine digestion, mental clarity, and ease of breath. The secrets of excellent health and longevity through martial practice are revealed over many years. Good, safe practices will be logical and in accord with medical knowledge and the ways of nature.

Organic Patterns

The great neo-Confucian scholar Zhu Xi [1130–1200] wrote of the inner workings of the Dao. He stated that we see its manifestations through vital energy [qi] along with a universal order called *li*. A study of this later concept offers great insight into how a martial art style looks and indicates the level of mastery an individual displays.

The origins of the character li include the characters for "jade," "field," and "earth." This had the meanings of "to cut jade, to mark out (field boundaries)." The symbolism of li therefore hints at underlying patterns, as displayed in a cross section of a jade piece, or in the order of a field as marked by its boundaries. We find such organic patterns in wood grain, flowing waters, the contours of terrain, a leaf's pattern, a trail of rising smoke, or fluctuating clouds. Together, vital energy and li created nature and ten thousand inherent patterns.

Can we find a pattern or order in our martial arts? Is there a guiding principle or organizational law that whispers to us on how we should develop our techniques? First, it seems apparent that we utilize a body structure that is designed by nature and operates by its own inherent laws. The body's structure offers us a great variety of ways we can orchestrate its components into martial techniques. The difficulty here lies within our present aptitude for doing this most efficiently. If our concepts are faulty, so will our techniques be faulty. How can we know that our techniques are in accord with a natural pattern? When we realize a fault, it is telling us to adapt and try another method. We can't stagnate. We move on, discovering, learning, and correcting.

Dive into a swift flowing river and swim against the current. Keep swimming, but gradually change the direction —0 to 45 degrees, to 90, to 135, then to 180—finally swimming directly with the current. In every case, you would be swimming, but the amount of difficulty changes. Most martial art practitioners, including teachers, are actually fighting themselves to some degree while performing their techniques: bone and joint alignment may be slightly off, their striking angle may not be optimal, or a push may not be directed to the proper target. Many such faults can be found, all executed to a greater or lesser degree of the ideal technique.

Techniques that are the furthest from the ideal are the most difficult to perform, or are just impossible to do with any success—like being totally exhausted and swimming against the river's current. Techniques made in accord with li—the ideal pattern of the movement—are the easiest to perform and result in total success. Li is not seen and experienced solely in physical movement. It also involves the timing of the technique. It can't be made too late or too early. Different skill levels shown in martial movements bear heavily on the limited awareness and abilities of each individual.

Today we can see all around China a myriad of martial systems: close-in or far-ranging tactics, hard or soft approaches, close or wide stances, wrestling versus standing, leaning or upright . . . and the descriptive list goes on. The results we see are the attempts by masters to develop their systems. How close do they come to the natural patterns and laws of kinetics?

The quality of their arts reflects the li of martial technique.

Weapons and Empty-Hand Practice

Empty-hand practice is very common because any routine or technique can be done at nearly any time and any place. However, for military, security, and law enforcement, the use of weapons predominates. Depending on the objectives and duties, the most familiar weapons include the spear [*qiang*], broadsword [*dao*], staff [*gun*], and—the gentleman of weapons —the straight double-edged sword [jian]. Because of the size and lethality of such weapons, practicing with them is often confined to special training areas, such as at a military academy. We can take a brief look at the fascinating relationship and parallels between weapons and empty-hand practice.

From my experience, most teachers prefer that one start martial studies with bare-hand techniques and routines. Combat theory is introduced along with the fundamentals of practice. With time the student should achieve good overall body coordination and a solid repertoire of fighting skills. With this background in bare-hand training, it is an easy transition to employ any weapon with fair competence. After you gain familiarity with a weapon's use for defense and attack, the weapon begins to feel like an extension of your body.

Many of the bare-hand techniques transfer directly into weapons techniques—however, some don't. The size, shape, and weight of the weapon reveal their own secrets to the student. A curved weapon, such as the broadsword, teaches one how to cut horizontally while following the waist's turning, keeping blade pressure against the enemy's body while making the turn. The straight sword teaches the subtle cuts that can be made while effortlessly withdrawing, as while drawing the blade under an opponent's wrist. The spear teaches one to extend one's energy through the shaft to the target. The staff has its own way of imparting the value of yin and yang through use of its opposite ends for attacking and defending.

If practitioners have good skills in bare-hand martial arts, they will adjust to the additional length of weapons and the resulting fighting distance. Just as we can sense an adversary's movement whenever arms touch, we can also feel through a weapon that is touching the opponent's weapon and know his intensions. We can know how he will initiate an attack before it is fully executed. The opponent's gates, opened and closed, are visible. Of course, it is only when one has a high level of skills in bare-hand techniques that these skills will be manifested in use of weapons.

When people are drafted or enlisted in the military, they often do not have any martial art experience. They are assigned to specific regiments and given weapons needed by particular units. Their training is often short term. As would be expected, they learn only basic techniques and their level of skill is low.

For serious practitioners, experience with bare-hand and weapons techniques provides insights into the deepest aspects of the richness of a martial system. This knowledge is impossible to convey to those who have not put the time and effort into the actual practices involved. Those with experience see how the rotating thrust of a spear operates the same as when one catches an opponent's wrist and elbow, then twists the forearm into the unforgiving breaking angle. How the energy transmits from the legs to the shoulders for the common punch chambered at the hip is the same as when holding the straight sword at one's side. Such insights make learning easier and easier. Those with time and talent can become fluent with an array of weaponry.

The Teacher's Effects

We've seen how children inherit their physical features from their parents. They inherit much more, including a local dialect, preferences for certain foods, and even manners and ways of thought. Traditional martial arts instruction calls for a close teacher-student bond and the effects can stay for a lifetime.

Anyone who desires to study a martial art may be limited by the number of masters living within close proximity. Another hurdle is the formality when approaching a potential teacher. Is the teacher a relative or a longtime family acquaintance? If accepted, the new student may become a decades-long disciple. Depending on the master's background, the curriculum may be limited to specific branches of a style, or to a complete system. The bare-hand practices may focus on specific aspects, such as striking, throwing, wrestling, locking, or kicking. Rarely do masters include all of these. The same with weapons. Some teachers may teach the straight sword only, while others can include a dozen weapons as part of the system.

Within the system being taught are unique ways of moving that the teacher imparts to each student, in addition to what the student learns by observation over the years. We need to remember that teachers possess different levels of skills and abilities. This means the student will inherit and reflect the teacher's style, including any flaws. When an unknown person performs a martial routine, others can immediately infer who must be the performer's teacher. They recognize the inherited style, as a son inherits the looks of his father.

Over time, movements become habit. As years pass, a senior disciple may figure out a better way to perform a technique, or he may learn from another teacher. But habits are very difficult to change. This is why it is extremely important to study with the best teacher available. Oftentimes, bad habits endure, and no amount of time or work will bring improvement.

In my case, being from a small town, my original teacher was a wonderful man who treated me as his own son. He taught the best he could. As I advanced, he later introduced me to another teacher, giving me permission to study and accept a new master. Because of my work as a painter, I traveled to some major cities and had the opportunity to learn with others who knew my former teachers. How I practice today reflects all teachers I have met, some having more influence than others. Much like one person may have physical characteristics similar to those of different relatives, you can notice different traits in my martial art.

We should make improvements in our art whenever we become aware that a fault exists and a correction is needed. Often the refinement is difficult and requires much time and work. Another aspect of martial arts study proves to be even more difficult to recognize and change. This involves theory. For example, our teacher may believe that a striking technique should be thrown from a strong base, toes holding onto the ground with legs tensed to resemble a building's stone foundation. From one perspective, this theory makes sense and is often used by the less experienced. It can be set aside when one discovers a better way of doing the technique. We continually try to improve the martial theory and our practice. The greatest hope is that the student will eventually surpass the teacher.

Now, as a teacher who has the honor of wearing a full head of frost-white hair, I can look back on my days training under great masters. Only later in life did I realize that I neglected to show my full appreciation for their time, teachings, and friendship. I was young and shortsighted. I was too self-centered. I didn't do enough to help my teachers in their later years. I could have run some errands or done household chores for them. I should have sat at their feet to keep them company and asked details about their youth.

Although I failed to fully express my gratitude—only decades later I came to realize just how immense it would be—I'm sure they knew my only fault was being young. I didn't realize that each day we were together would impart meaningful thoughts and feelings that will stay embedded in my core until my last days in this earthly realm. The situation finds parallel in the relationship between parents and offspring.

We often find it too late to do and say what we should have at an earlier time. If we were only more aware of the significance teachers and parents have on our lives. What they have given us came from lives they lived—despite their own faults and years of struggle and hardship. Their willingness to spend time together is an altruistic gift, one that allows us to absorb the wisdom and skills they have honed over decades.

"The Three Vinegar Tasters," Laozi, Buddha, and Confucius. After sipping some vinegar, their faces reflect their philosophies of life in the mundane world.

By Kano Isen'in, c. 1802–1816, Honolulu Museum of Art. Public domain, via Wikimedia Commons.

The Learning Continuum

The most noted martial art systems have been built upon centuries of trial and error and are embodied in the knowledge and combative skills of the contemporary great masters. The rich martial systems—long boxing [*changquan*]; soft fist [*taijiquan*]; mantis and other Northern styles; the five family styles of the South, particularly those of the Eight Great Schools in the sacred mountains; and those centered in the great cities—all have curricula of great scope.

Whenever fate brings an aspiring person to the gate of

one of the great martial systems, the new member will have preconceived ideas of what he will learn over the next years and perhaps decades. Perhaps he wishes to study martial arts to fulfill a fantasy to live the chivalrous and heroic life as a character from the novel *Outlaws of the Marsh*? The student has high hopes of becoming an invincible warrior who can fly over the heads of foes and defeat them with a dazzling display of sword skills. Of course, there are many reasons to begin studies.

With time, the new student realizes that advanced students view the martial arts in greater depth. Others of more experience have an even greater perspective. It is like a country person who arrives in Beijing for the first time and is overwhelmed at the sheer sea of people, buildings, and cultural gems. On his own, he'd surely get lost in this wondrous Celestial City. To get a decent introduction, he needs a tour guide, someone familiar with the city and the major attractions. However, even a tour guide may not know the doorways and alleys through the complex *hutong* (衚 衕) neighborhoods. Only a longtime resident would know the histories of each building and the individuals who populated them. Some know even the ghosts who linger there.

The beginner student is much like the country bumpkin entering the glorious capital, and the guide is an experienced student who extends a hand. The grandmaster knows the whole city and its every brick.

Students who have joined a martial arts family stand on a line that extends from them through the more advanced students up to the grandmaster. Along that line, seasoned students can look back with clear understanding of how novices think and feel as they start their practice. When the new student raises his hand to ask a question, the advanced student already knows what it is. At the same time, beginning students only have a very blurry vision of what the more advanced students have experienced in their studies. Easy to look back. Impossible to look ahead. Even those who have lived in the Forbidden City all their lives do not know the mysteries of all 9,999 rooms.

Moving from Time to the Timeless

Some Daoists and Buddhists who live in the mountain temples include a specific method to develop their fighting arts based on the eight trigrams. Stemming from taiji, yin-yang, and five phases, the eight trigrams offer many secrets for a martial artist. One of the more obscure teachings derived from the eight trigrams offers practitioners a way to enter a state where there is no time.

We thank our first emperor, Fuxi, for the eight trigrams, which he devised as he contemplated the Changes nearly four thousand years ago. He took the broken (yin) and solid (yang) lines to form the trigrams: ☰ ☱ ☲ ☳ ☴ ☵ ☶ ☷. These symbols have many connotations, one of them being the mode of movement. Some mountain recluses walk along in combative postures, following an imaginary circle on the ground, which is marked by eight points corresponding to the trigrams. Following the circle and making changes in this direction allows the practitioner to learn footwork for moving around opponents while utilizing a splendid repertoire of combat techniques.

One walking practice involves two practitioners who position themselves on opposite sides of the circle and begin walking. While moving at the same tempo, they focus their eyes on each other's chest. During the walk, they also hold their hands toward the center of the circle, one hand just below eye level and the other hand at stomach level. They initially walk at a slow speed and very gradually increase the speed to a full run. Looks like a tornado of dust!

When visiting my friendly reclusive monks, they invited me to try this practice. As the tempo increased, it became disquieting, but as we continued, I seemed to glide along, faster and faster. Everything around us became a blur of colors: the ground like a cloud, the sides ripples made of nature's hues.

Within this vortex I found myself facing the other in complete stillness. My friend slowly reached out with one hand to touch my lead hand. How was this slow movement possible while walking the circle at such a high-speed? Is this the same mental state that results from a few pipes of opium, the new drug the British import here from India?

It took some days to actually realize the value of my lesson that day: when we move in harmony with an opponent, time slows down between us, even while all around us is in chaos. It seems to give ample time to respond to any attack. There is serenity at the center of the whirlwind. However, freeze while the other is in movement, and time returns—and then movement arrives like a lightening bolt. Ever since that day walking circles in the mountains, I always coordinate and blend my movements with the opponent's in any two-person practice. Of course, you don't need to move in circles to do this. Blend with your opponent in any direction, which takes more practice to learn how to stick with him even when he may move in various unpredictable directions. This requires much relaxation throughout the body and keen awareness.

Telltale Signs

A darkening of clouds. Some flashes of light in the sky. A stirring breeze. All these are indicators of a gathering storm. We learn to read the signs and prepare for the event. Good to learn the telltale signs lest we get split in half by a lightning bolt. Same with the combative arts. We learn to read the telltale signs and prepare for any attack.

The initial movement of an opponent can indicate which direction he will go. If one is familiar with an assortment of techniques, the movement also foretells which techniques can be made from changing postures. Of course, this implies being aware of the opponent's overall body position, where the hands are positioned, for example. Knowing the body posture and the direction of movement informs us about possible attacking

71

methods. We can discuss some of the more obvious signs.

Some masters believe it best to not take any fighting stance when confronted. The stance usually shows the style you have studied. If an adversary is familiar with the style, he will know the methods of defense and attack. Rather than lifting the hands forward, say into a praying mantis posture, he may simply let the hands relax downward in a comfortable standing posture, hidden by long sleeves. So, as a defense, it is often beneficial to try not to show any telltale signs of potential martial abilities. We cloak our combative abilities while observing the potential in any attacker.

The direction in which an opponent wishes to go quickly shows in his feet. Moving forward, the back heel starts to rise from the ground. Moving backward, the front toes start to rise. If the left foot is in front, turning it 45 degrees to the left allows the back leg to kick forward. If the front left foot turns nearly 180 degrees right, it predicts a back kick or a backhand strike. Foot positions foreshadow the potential for a linear or a circular attack. Regarding forward kicks, watch for the direction of the knee, as it points to where the foot will follow.

The hand positions are certainly key indicators for predicting how an opponent may attack. A hand held high usually moves down, and vice versa. Same for a hand positioned to the left or right. Any fully extended arm will eventually move back toward the center. But an easily perceived indicator of arm movement can be observed in shoulder movement. For example, we can imagine an opponent standing with his left side forward. If his left shoulder starts to turn back, we know the right shoulder will turn forward, which predicts a right-handed strike utilizing the hand or perhaps the elbow. Movements from one side of the body give telltale signs of what possible techniques can be executed from the opposite side. So, we remain astute observers of any shoulder movements, since they indicate what both arms are doing.

Subtler than the turning of the shoulders is the turning of the waist. A slight turn of the waist may initiate movements in the arms and legs. As the hips move, alignment of the skeletal system changes, allowing some techniques to be utilized and keeping others from any possibility of being used.

Despite such telltale signs, hinted by the hands, shoulders, waist, or feet, it is not easy to read or to predict what techniques will actually follow. Attackers also have false starts and utilize feints. We must be aware of this and know of our own ability to read the signs properly. It is like learning a foreign language, where a beginner will make many mistakes. With time and practice, one improves. For the highly skilled martial artist, reading telltale signs becomes instinctive, allowing the master to arrive before the attacker's movement.

Inspiration

The characters for "inspiration" (*linggan*) convey layers of meanings. *Ling* may show that thinking of our ancestral spirits or a thing of value can drench one with inspiration. The second character, *gan*, shows that when the heart is stirred, it drives one to act with conviction, hence to speak up, fight for, or show affection. There are times when we lose interest in our practice for short periods, and perhaps we have thoughts to stop practicing altogether. How can we find the inspiration to return?

It certainly inspires me to practice martial arts when I think of my past masters who shared their time and special knowledge of the combat arts. Hopefully we all have a teacher who inspires us, or know of masters who do. How they move, their depth of knowledge, and their respectful character should nudge us to regular practice. Friends and fellow students may give us support through words of encouragement and by sharing the joys of camaraderie in the arts.

It is also helpful to look back at what we've accomplished so far in our discipline. The time and effort put into practice shows in improved technical skills, and clear progress shows in the achievements. It also manifests in improved health and well-being. By learning a practical system of self-defense, we develop an appreciation for the aesthetics of movement. We find joy in creating a living, moving art.

Wonderful memories arise of special places where one has practiced, such as in quiet temple courtyards, misty Daoist hermitages, or along a tranquil lake. The early mornings, while rising energies for the day stimulate the atmosphere, are especially conducive to a rewarding practice. We think of practicing in such locations, and we look forward to the future.

Even when masters and kindred souls are not nearby to inspire, we can read the writings of masters to refresh our desire to practice. Some excellent works of fiction can do this too. The writing does not necessarily need to focus on martial arts. Often, short philosophical discourses or a one-sentence quote can spark the flame of inspiration.

We find meaning from past and present masters, as well as the desire to become proficient in the fighting arts for self-defense and protecting loved ones in case a threatening situation occurs. We improve or maintain health through a balanced discipline shared with like minds. A caution is to not practice to the extreme, which can exhaust one to the point where it becomes difficult to continue.

Whenever you lack the will to maintain a regular practice, the above ideas should inspire you to return to the path. There are many reasons that make our practice meaningful. Perhaps the strongest impetus comes from a clear vision of our goals and the expected rewards from the time and effort we put into practice.

Spontaneous Naturalness

In the *Daodejing*, Laozi used the compound word *ziran*. It implies "spontaneous naturalness." What a wonderful concept! And a concept so befitting of Daoism. Ziran refines the usual mode of trying or making something natural. Ziran cannot be contrived. We need to let ourselves move naturally.

There is nothing artificial about it. It is purely spontaneous. For the martial artist, we should never pretend we are moving naturally.

An often-used metaphor of this naturalness is an uncarved block of wood. In its original, unadulterated state, wood has its own inherent qualities. It is a simple piece of wood when untouched. It is being wood. If carved, it can be a spoon or another tool. For combat, this metaphor hints at how we usually make movements and techniques rather than let them flow naturally. This seems to be a common learning progression. A master shows a movement, and the student imitates it. The student tries to move as the teacher moves. The student places his body postures and movements, thinking, remembering, and trying to copy the teacher's form. After mimicking the teacher well enough, the student hopes to reach another learning stage.

After imitating the teacher's movements and perhaps after some years of practice, the student will not need to think so much about the many details of each movement. Thinking disrupts movement much like a chisel gouges wood. Usually, martial artists think, plan, connive, and try to trick an opponent —unnecessary mental activities that prevent any natural movement. Thinking takes time, and in combat, time is of the essence. Therefore, spontaneity is crucial. In the martial arts, and likewise in calligraphy, the highly skilled seek ziran —spontaneous naturalness. This concept couples nicely with the concept of wuwei, doing nothing against the Dao, nothing against naturalness.

The great benefit of being spontaneous is speed. As an opponent strikes, the defender is instantly moving—perhaps even ahead of the opponent's attack. The great advantage of being natural is that the body can move in its optimal way, without flaw. If you can move with ziran—spontaneity and naturalness together—you will represent the highest level of combat movement. To attain this level requires inborn abilities nurtured by years of training. To observe a master martial artist or calligrapher perform in this way is to witness the miraculous, a blessing, and rare proof that the ziran theory can be put into practice.

Help Your Attacker

The words "combat," "fight," "battle," and "hostilities" conjure up the idea of intense, violent confrontation. Whenever two powerful forces clash, damage is done. Usually, the more formidable person or group emerges victorious. Since this is the norm, individuals, brigands, police, and great imperial armies strive to build their strength. They exercise, train, and create new weaponry in order to build an overbearing force. But there is another way—to fight without fighting. Laozi wrote

> Everyone knows that the yielding
> overcomes the stiff,
> and the soft overcomes the hard.
> Yet no one applies this knowledge.

Resist with strength or yield with softness? Hardwood is praised for its strength. When a hardwood tree is covered with weighty ice during the winter, its branches crack, break, and fall to the ground. In contrast, hollow bamboo bends under pressure, sometimes all the way to the ground, but it does not break. As the ice slowly melts, bamboo springs back into an upright position. A symbol of moral uprightness and resistance, bamboo is very strong, yet very flexible. It is commonly used in construction for high scaffolding, as well as in buildings. Bamboo's qualities can give insights into the martial arts.

Rather than resist a push, move with it. Rather than retreat from a pull, go with it. By moving with the attacker, no tension can build. The attacker's own force can cause him to lose balance and put him in awkward positions. Experiment with yielding, and many advantages become apparent. If an aggressor tries to shove you with both hands, meet his hands with yours, and pull to help him continue forward. While you step back, he'll fall down—or you can meet his forward movement with a knee to the solar plexus. Let him pull your wrist, move in the direction pulled, and use a shoulder push to knock him away. He will be surprised!

Developing this effortless power takes much time. Not many pursue this method. Of those who do, very few can embody the principles into real application. It is counterintuitive. However, once you feel the practicality of "helping the attacker," those skills become the superior method for combat.

Water Ways

Martial arts are movement. Water is another Daoist metaphor that is especially helpful for understanding movement. In the *Daodejing*, Laozi writes: "Supreme good is like water. Water greatly benefits all things, without conflict." Because water is fluid, soft, and pliant, it maintains its qualities even when coming against other objects. It overcomes the hard, much like its flow wears down rock. We see that many martial art styles include techniques that flow like water.

A boulder falls from a hillside into a river, and water moves around it. A formidable opponent may stand before us like a human boulder. To confront him head-on is suicide, so we flow around him. He may strike forward, so we step to the left, blocking his forward strike with a left hand, simultaneously turning like an eddy, striking to the back of his head with a right elbow. Many techniques flow around any direct confrontation, usually by moving to the left or right. This can take the defense to the sides, but also behind the opponent. Some techniques flow completely around the opponent, 360 degrees. Other techniques move to the side or back, then reverse direction.

Water moves around and also under objects. Because it seeks the low position, it is a metaphor for being humble. Some low-moving techniques are utilized when an opponent attacks high. As the yang energy rushes forward, a defender uses flowing yin energy to move into the lower space, often to strike the attacker's lower body or to slide underneath him for a throw.

Thinking of the liquid nature of water and imagining how it moves gives us many examples that can be applied in combative techniques. We can easily visualize the large movements, such as moving to the left and right of an oncoming attack. This is like seeing a river torrent glide around a protruding slab. But water also moves in waves, twisting and turning, and penetrating. It moves in currents, large and small. One's body parts can imitate water movements, even in very small maneuvers. We see this in escaping attempted grabs or locks when the hand or arm can be pliant enough and moved appropriately.

Whenever pushed, pressed, or hit, water simply yields, moves around, encompasses. While the yielding nature of water is of great practical use for defense, it is of equal value for attacking. It has the power of a tidal wave, rolling directly into an opponent or swerving into him from the sides. It can press down with its weight or draw someone off balance by withdrawing a space. For defense, being like water, one cannot be hit or grabbed. For attacking, a stream of techniques can be executed to drown an opponent.

Seeing Targets

Invited to an exquisite banquet, we see a fine display of foods set out on the table. Such a wonderful variety! Despite all the shapes, textures, and colors, your eyes are drawn to the familiar delicacies. You try the spicy Szechuan noodles, cutting the long noodles in half with chopsticks and picking a peanut up to your mouth to taste the flavor of red chili and oil. Then with your chopsticks, you poke into a West Lake fish in dark vinegar sauce, spreading the sticks to split it into bite-sized pieces. Scoop some white rice from a small bowl to cleanse the palate before grabbing a Northern-style dumpling dipped in sesame oil. To see the correlations between this food display and martial arts, we may need a few cups of distilled sorghum clear white liquor.

You'll remember the chopstick techniques used in the preceding paragraph: cut, pick, poke, split, and scoop. These techniques are similar to those used in the fighting arts, such as strike, grab, split, chop, sweep . . . and there's more than just this correspondence. Years of daily meals have given us experience so that we can now quickly notice what food to select and what appropriate technique we will use to eat it. Given our great familiarity with the utensil and the types of food, we move smoothly, utilizing many techniques, according to desire.

A highly experienced chef can be compared to a martial art master. They both see what lies before them and act spontaneously to achieve their goals. The martial artist doesn't only see an opponent; he sees strengths and weaknesses in his presence. Why attack a strong point when the chance of success is very slim? Even without making conscious analysis, we may notice that certain targets beg for attack: a straightened leg or arm invites a joint break; an unbalanced, speedy retreat is convenient to push; a poorly aligned punch is easy to neutralize; a high strike leaves a low opening; and an easily grabbed kick facilitates a throw. Regardless of how an opponent postures, there are weak points exposed. Even the strongest posture can be toppled with a one-finger push at the appropriate point.

Seeing the weak and strong points of an opponent is a special ability. In order to take advantage of this awareness, one must also factor in timing and ever-changing maneuvers. The potential for success is low for those lacking experience and skills. Their vision is clouded by limited knowledge of martial techniques and not being astute enough to accurately assess a combat situation to their own advantage. It seems a master can intuit what target to attack using techniques—all while making it appear effortless. It reminds me of when I was a young child, watching my first martial arts master so accurately picking small peanuts out of a bowl. The ease he exhibited greatly magnified my clumsy use of chopsticks, missing the peanuts or flicking them sideways through the air.

Elbows Moving the Wrong Way

I like the idiom "The elbow turns the wrong way." This phrase carries the meaning that one favors an outsider instead of someone on one's own side. The martial family—based on familial ties, very close friendships, and trust—is a tight group dedicated to the secrets of a combat tradition. The most important knowledge of the art is kept close and not given to any outsiders. These high-level teachings are never demonstrated publically. Some cryptic writings have been preserved within families. If ever made known to outsiders, pain and suffering would result, given the possibility that the knowledge could be used unscrupulously against the family or others.

Of course, the idiom in question points to the obvious fact that moving an arm beyond its natural extension brings pain to the joint. A good martial artist is careful never to extend the arm to its maximum. If reaching or striking outward, he immediately pulls back. The same precaution is given to kicking methods. My teachers would advise that the arm or leg be returned twice as fast as the outward movement. This may be impossible, but the counsel only stresses the importance of safeguarding the joints.

Many problems arise when the arm movements are made with too much muscular tension, and solely in an individualized manner. The elbow loses its function to bend and can be easily damaged by fast movements, by applying combat techniques, or by an attack. The word "bend" in Chinese includes two characters for silk, offering a good image to emulate. Letting the elbows relax allows them to bend, twist, and buckle naturally. A flexible elbow is difficult to secure in an armlock.

One way to loosen the arms in martial practice is to allow them to move with the waist. Turn in any direction, and the waist turns the shoulders—and the arms follow. This is most easily seen in the ward-off movement, resembling one who reaches into a bag of grain on the left side and throws it with an arm swing to the right. This movement is very common because we utilize it in many ways, in blocking, striking, or throwing. Of great importance here is that the movement not be made solely with the forearm. Done with the power of the legs and directed by the waist, the arms should be loose enough that the elbow moves freely outward with the forearm and hand. The same principle applies in the reverse direction. Let the elbows move to the left or right along with the forearms. Watch that the elbows are not held into the body by stiffness.

One exercise that greatly helps keep the elbows flexible can be done against a wall. Assume a bow stance with your left foot forward. Extend your left arm, placing the back of it lightly against the wall. Don't fully extend the arm. Shift slowly toward the wall, and let the elbow move downward with gravity. You'll see and feel slack in the arm, much as would occur if the arm were a rope or a length of silk. Retreat in the same manner, keeping the back of the hand lightly against the wall. Do this ten times or so to relax and get the feeling of what is happening.

A variation of this exercise adds a turn. Rather than simply shifting toward the wall, shift and turn the waist left, which brings you to face the wall. The palm will naturally rotate, but be sure to keep the hand in the same place. You should finish the approach comfortably, with both shoulders an equal distance from the wall. When very relaxed, the left elbow follows the waist-shoulder movement to the left. This will flip the hand over so the palm faces downward. When you advance, the right shoulder comes closer to the left hand. The left hand and right shoulder point in the same direction, to the right. Some say this is like *embrace the moon*, the left arm resting over the globe. It is practical when an adversary grabs your wrist.

It stays in one place while the rest of the body moves.

The above exercises have many practical uses in combat. For example, if you strike out with your right hand and your opponent grabs your wrist, you can move quickly toward your opponent to strike with your left hand. In the movement, he would not sense your forward motion, since there is no tension in your right arm. If the attacker pushes against the relaxed arm, your body remains unaffected, free to move and counter.

Another very practical application is using the elbow for blocking or deflecting. For example, stand with your right foot to the front, your right arm relaxed and straight out in the direction of the opponent's left shoulder. Seeing an opening, he may strike toward your chest. Some pull their right arm to the front to block. This works, but it creates unnecessary tensions and slows any counter. Without force, shift to the back leg while turning the waist left. If the right arm is relaxed, the turn will bring the forearm and elbow left against the incoming attack. You will deflect the punch safely to your side. A counter, such as *snake darts out*, with the right fist, is easy, and you are in perfect position to execute it.

In the movements described above, we see how the elbows and arms do not have to be forced into positions. They move with the waist, to the left, right, up, and down. Experiment with this idea, and you'll find that the arms, elbows, and hands move defensively and offensively by the movement of the waist. As a sample, try stork spreads wings. The arms should not move on their own. The left hand moves downward and slightly to the left, as one sinks and turns; the right hand raises as one rises and turns slightly right. The waist directs the arms. Don't push with arm power. The power comes from the legs.

Techniques and Distance

Since the times of the Yellow Emperor, thousands of tools have been invented, made for specific jobs. In warfare on land and sea, the array of weaponry is tremendous. We have chariots, artillery, crossbows, incendiary bombs, chains, whips, rope darts, swords, spears, guns, and more. Some are ancient and still practical; other weapons reflect technical advancements and foreign influences. For an individual martial art practitioner, the standard weapons are practical for personal self-defense as well as for exercise.

Some styles utilize a long pole in practice, a weapon roughly double the length of a regular spear. The pole is heavy. Lifting and shaking it require full-body movement. In the old days, long poles could be used to knock a driver from a chariot. The spear continues to be a valued weapon. It keeps opponents at bay. For closer-range fighting, we have the staff, sectional staffs, and swords. At even closer range, knives, hooks, and clubs are useful. From cannonball to dagger, the fighting range varies greatly, and an extensive scope and variety of weapons cover the distances.

For bare-handed combat, we are left with the human body and its innate weapons. The legs are most powerful and provide the greatest reach. If an opponent throws a punch, a defensive kick will arrive first. However, kicks are fairly easy to block, deflect, or evade safely from their trajectory. They also open areas for counterattack, such as the groin.

Coming in closer range, the hands become primary weapons for offense and defense. Once this range between two fighters is made, even an incremental advance allows the use of knees and elbows. The possible combinations using these close-range weapons are seemingly infinite. A flurry may be neutralized by moving away, outside of range, or moving even closer together. When two bodies are at their closest proximity, even the arms become difficult to use. Now the body's weapons work under the restraint of limited space. The head butt is commonly used. You may see advanced practitioners use other techniques, such as striking with the shoulders, shifting weight, and attacking pressure points.

The techniques for long, medium, and close ranges can all be used when moving closer to an opponent. For example, a low kick can be followed by a punch, an elbow strike, and then a finishing technique, such as a push made with the hip or a throw. When moving away from an opponent, such movements can be made in reverse order. An example could be using a shoulder strike to knock an opponent back, allowing enough room for an elbow strike to the head, shifting away while throwing a backhand to the temple, and then ending with a back kick to the stomach. Defending and attacking, the body's weapons fold in and out as suitable to the situation. It's all a matter of using the right tool at the right time, according to the distance.

Mental and Optical Illusions

Whenever we watch a master perform, what we think we see may not be what is really happening. An arm circles around. A foot turns. A strike moves straight out to the front, using the side of the hand. The wrist bends as it cranks an opponent's wrist. The eyes focus attention on the lead hand making the technique. In all such cases, we should know for sure what is being done, why it's being done, and how it's being done.

I watched someone practicing *sea-bottom probe*. With one hand over the other, he brought both hands downward to the front. This movement is commonly used to pull an opponent's hand and body forward and down, often using a wristlock. He told me this was what he was doing.

"OK," I said, "try it with me so I can see how it works."

It didn't. His hand positions were perfect, but his legs were pushing upward, lifting his back, which neutralized his arm movement downward. As a result . . . we stood there holding hands.

Why would he lift his back in *sea-bottom probe*? Whoever showed him the movement did not show him the regular application and had a variation in mind. The opponent is not standing in front. In this variation, the technique is used when the opponent is attacking from behind, or you turn your back to fit in against him. It is an excellent throw, sinking while grabbing the opponent's wrist and arm, then raising the back and directing his arm downward. A very common throw, but the practitioner didn't even know where the opponent was positioned. He didn't realize the function of the technique.

In another case, a practitioner was standing upright with his feet shoulder width apart. He turned his shoulders 90 degrees to the left while shifting to the right leg, his right hand pushing left. He said he was pushing an imaginary opponent on his left side. Again, this doesn't work. The technique is not yang, but yin. It is useful when someone attempts to push or strike at you from the front. When you turn the body and shift to the right leg, you avoid the attack, and the right hand or forearm comes against the attacker's arm—a counter can then be easily executed. Again, the practitioner didn't even know from which direction the attack was made.

Many optical illusions occur in the simplest of movements. We can use *brush knee, twist step* as an example, starting from a front stance with the right foot forward, left arm at front, and right arm down by the side.

(1) We may see a master shift back onto the left leg and turn the front foot right. A closer observation shows that the front foot did not move on its own, but the change was totally generated by turning the waist.

(2) We also notice movements of the left and right arms. A close observation shows that the waist movement to the right causes both arms to move.

(3) Then the master steps out with his left leg, blocks downward with his left hand, and raises his right arm to the back. These may look like three separate movements, but all are done simultaneously under the powers of the waist. How? Sinking on the right leg allows the left leg to step out—the lower he sinks, the longer the stride. Sinking starts the left hand downward. It may seem counterintuitive, but this also

starts the upward movement of the right hand! Test this by holding the right hand stationary. As the body sinks to a lower position, it appears as if the right hand has risen, even though the hand hasn't moved an inch. But, if the arm is relaxed, the turning and sinking movements are what set the arm in motion.

(4) This sequence ends by shifting about 70 percent of the weight onto the left leg and pushing with the right arm. Again, close observation shows that the right hand is not pushing on its own. It utilizes the waist turn and leg shift to provide momentum and power to the push. The waist turn also motivates the final movement of the left hand and a turn of the left toes to the front.

When watching their teacher, new students of the martial arts usually notice individual parts of the overall movement. Therefore, they practice by moving individual parts of their bodies to make a technique. It takes time for them to see the body moving as a whole in a synchronistic fashion. It may take some years to understand and more years to put into effect. There are many possible variations to movements. One technique can have ten applications. As stated above, we should know for sure what is being done, why it's being done, and how it's being done.

Power behind the Punch

The straight punch is the fundamental technique of attack in the martial arts. All styles employ it, although the effective quality varies among practitioners. There are a number of factors that determine the effectiveness, but perhaps the most important factor is the degree of tension in the throwing arm. How much tension should be in the fist, with each finger curled in to support the structure? How much tension should come from the biceps? Each practitioner performs according to his or her understanding of where the power originates.

Many masters I've met, experts of various styles, share some common beliefs in how a basic punch is thrown. All have discussed the importance of moving the hips and shoulders, and shifting the weight. They stress proper alignment from the elbow to the fist so the skeletal parts move in the same direction as not to cause breaks or fractures to the one throwing the punch.

I unexpectedly found a metaphor that helps explain the arm alignment and source of power in the basic punch. It was demonstrated to me while interviewing Manchu and Chinese bow and arrow makers working for the imperial guards. I was accompanying Giuseppe Castiglione to help him interview archers for some paintings, including images of the Qianlong Emperor (r. 1736–1796) himself, Prince Yinli (1697–1738), and the hero mounted archer Maqang. The bow and arrow makers provided accurate information and details for the paintings, including a number of military and hunting scenes. Regarding archery, the military standard draw weights for the bow ranged from 70 to 100 pounds, but some experts would draw up to nearly 240 pounds with 52-inch arrows.

An analogy appears between the punching arm and arrow. The arrow is nocked to the bowstring held by the fingers and rests against the bow on the other hand. As the string is drawn, immense power is created by the composite recurve bow. The great effectiveness of the arrow is derived from the speed and resulting power from releasing the string. We can support this analogy with another, that of Chen family's second routine, which they call cannon fist. The cannonball sits in the barrel. What gives it destructive force is the gunpowder.

Here we see that the fist can sit chambered at the hip in a relaxed, natural state, as the arrow sits in its nocked position. The arrow is ready to receive power from the taut string, just as the cannonball rests in the bore of the barrel, ready to receive power from ignited gunpowder. The arm is propelled forward by the power of the body, especially from the rear leg.

Then added speed and force come from shifting and turning the hips and shoulders. The stance from which the punch is most often thrown is called the "bow stance." A target absorbs the power of the punch. During practice, one must be careful to avoid overextending, as it is easy to injure the elbow joint. Usually tension is required to stop the punch, but it is not necessary to throw the punch. The knuckles of the fist do not get any harder by clenching. Proper alignment, utilization of the sources of power, and delivery are the only requirements. Let the arrow and cannonball fly! Let the fist fly!

Principles for Fighting and Health

Theory manifests in practice. Many practicing a martial art embody a theory they believe will make them strong and effective. They may place iron rings around their forearms to strengthen them during training. They may do hundreds of push-ups on their knuckles to callus them, or on their fingertips to imitate the claws of an eagle or tiger. They may repeatedly drag a heavy stone thirty feet by a rope tied to their testicles to attain "iron eggs," or punch their jewels by hand or with a wooden battering ram. They believe this prepares them for combat and the possibility of being kicked in the testicles. Some just retract the testicles from the scrotum into the groin to keep them protected.

In contrast to the above methods, we have others who employ a very different theory in their practices for health and longevity. A common thread is the cultivation of relaxation. Movements are practiced to nurture the body's systems without causing any short- or long-term injuries.

The variety of methods utilized in martial arts and health training are often very distinctly different, while many schools use a blend of yang-dominant training for combat and yin-dominant training for health. There are schools that do claim to use one theory for both combat and health training, but in most cases, differences show in their actual practice. For example, they may talk about being relaxed in their martial and health practices, but in reality they show an abundance of tension in combat, in contrast to their health exercises.

The idea that martial and health practices should be guided by the same principles may be very logical, but it is extremely difficult in practice. For example, the principle of relaxation is vital to nourishing health, but it takes much time and effort to bring about. Because of the nature of conflict, relaxation is even more difficult to maintain in the martial arts. Some fighting styles emphasize relaxation, and their fundamental training methods include slow movements to relieve muscular tensions, calm the mind, and sense any flaws in movement. Examples here are those of the Chen Family Village in their silky Long River Boxing style [taijiquan], and Daoist styles found in specific temples or as practiced by individual hermits. We must remember that the martial styles that emphasize slow, relaxed practice routines do not do so as the end goal. These styles utilize the slow in order to move fast. They utilize relaxation in order to move at optimal speed in the most natural way.

Main principles used for health exercises are relaxation, calmness, and balance, usually practiced in a slow, steady tempo. A goal for many martial artists is to embody the same principles in their practice. However, after we have comfortably practiced the combat movements, we should increase the speed. Here is the dilemma: how do we speed up while remaining relaxed and calm? Various schools of martial arts try to answer this question in various ways. Some foster a Zenlike mind to keep calm in the face of dangers. Physical relaxation is intimately tied to one's mental state.

An increase in speed also affects balance. Balancing in stationary postures and during slow movements is very different from maintaining balance during fast movement. For example, a flag hanging from a pole on a windless day acts differently during a windy day. However, the qualities of the flag itself have not changed. The dynamics involved affect the body movement much like wind affects the rippling flag. Compared with slow practice, fast movements extend the limbs, twisting and bending the spine to a greater degree, and human kinetics constantly adjust to the relationship of the changing forces, such as gravity.

In the gale of combat, one needs to move quickly and fluidly. A relaxed body lets this happen. Martial artists strive to reach the ideal of combat movement. Few reach the goal, while the majority continue to progress on the path of improvement.

Explosive Kicks and Strikes

Front, back, side, spinning . . . basic kicks are indispensable techniques for the martial arts and worth every effort to make them powerful and effective. New students face a common learning path: what part of the foot makes contact without getting hurt? How does power get to the foot? What parts of the body are used to perform the kick? And, of central importance, how can one maintain balance during the kick from beginning to end?

Watch new students prepare to kick from an empty stance [weight on the back leg, and the front leg positioned with the ball of the front foot on the ground] with a training bag in front. It takes some time for them to discover the correct distance so the foot hits the bag on target. When the foot makes contact with the bag, the rebounding force shakes the kicker, sometimes enough to cause him to fall off balance. The same repercussion can happen with hand strikes.

Many styles use a technique combining a kick and knife-hand strike from the same side of the body. For example, from a guard stance with the right foot forward, let the right hand and foot draw into the center then upward and outward with simultaneous strikes. Usually, beginners make this movement by pulling the right arm in toward the waist, then up to the chest, and pushing outward in a straight line. That is three movements to make the hand strike. More advanced students perform this technique in a circle, which is only one movement. Even with this improvement, there remains a problem with balancing, due to the rebounding effect.

One master offered suggestions on how to improve the techniques described above. Watching a student practicing his kicks, the master noticed that the student's back leg was stiff and almost straight. When the right foot hit the bag at nearly 90 degrees from his body, the power exerted simply pushed the student backward. If anyone stands upright on one leg, it is easy to push him over with one finger! The master offered this solution: sink downward on the left leg as the kicking leg draws in; then push upward on the stable leg while kicking. The center of balance does not change by the body moving down then up. The movement resembles an explosion: from the center the power radiates in all directions and maintains its center. The kicking leg expands outward with the whole body movement, then contracts with the whole body movement, settling at the base.

There is tremendous power in such a kick because it comes from the ground, with power emanating from the rooted leg as well as the kicking leg. In the earlier method, the kick was moving out 90 degrees from the body with nothing behind the body except air. Thus, no stabilization.

A knifehand strike is made with the same principles, but with an added detail. When the arm circles down, upward, and out, beginning students usually make the final movement straight toward the target, making a straight line. The strike should be made with a slight curve, which can make impact anywhere along that arc—upward on the chest or downward on the collarbone. If we think of the body as the center of a circle and the spine as the balance point, the circular movement maintains balance. This can be felt especially when the other hand is moving in the opposite direction of the striking hand. Power can be felt emanating from the ground as one rises and the hands explode outward.

Whenever practicing this type of explosive movement—

sinking and rising to maintain stability and adding power to strikes—be sure you don't come up too high. You must keep contact with the ground. Some styles sink into postures all the way to the ground and then rise to kick or strike. No need to sink so far, but even slightly sinking and rising will greatly enhance these types of kicks and strikes.

Personality and Personal Style

There is an extraordinary and wonderful collection of artworks in this capital of the Middle Kingdom. I'm most familiar with calligraphy and paintings that decorate the imperial collections, palaces, temples, and homes of mandarins. Every piece is distinct, reflecting the skills and minds of the creators. Some are certainly conservative, while others are quite eccentric. Artists like Yuan Jiang were influenced by the great masters of the past. We also see such artists as Zuo Yigui and Jiao Bingzhen adding Western techniques and perspectives in their works. Of course, Giuseppe Castiglione's profound influence reverberates with subtle European flair. What we see in all the best paintings is but a reflection of the skill, knowledge, and personality of each individual artist.

The martial arts are *arts*. So they also reflect the skill, knowledge, and personality of each individual artist. Combat knowledge and skills are passed down from masters, or even relative amateurs. Great masters are rare, and their systems stand out for their effectiveness and wide range of techniques. They are usually very selective of who they accept as disciples. There are relatively few who have the opportunity to learn these high-level systems. Many more study with teachers who are mediocre, who conveniently live in the vicinity and will accept them as students. As a result, the smorgasbord of styles represents great variation in quality.

The skills and knowledge of a particular martial art are passed from teacher to student and affect its outward characteristics. One more factor plays largely into the style, which is personality. At the Shaolin Temple, monks look at an individual's character to decide which animal style is suitable to study: snake, ape, monkey, tiger, dragon, or crane. In the major cities such as Beijing, Xi'an, Nanjing, Suzhou, and Guangdong, there are more opportunities to study than in small cities and villages. Individuals are drawn to styles that fit their personalities. Some styles rely on techniques of brute strength, and the practitioners portray that characteristic. Other styles are refined, utilizing principles of physics and sensitivity. Scholars and government officials prefer these styles. Then there are numerous styles that fall in between.

All martial art styles work. Some work better than others. As masters strive to improve their fighting skills, they work within the limitations of the arts they inherited, their knowledge, physical abilities, and personal dispositions. Much like people are drawn to particular painting styles, people have personal preferences for which combat style they practice. We are fortunate that the diversity presents us with the richness of Chinese martial traditions.

Solo Routines and Self-Defense

For centuries, masters have created and preserved martial art routines. Some are short, consisting of a few techniques, while others are long, with perhaps one hundred or more techniques. The routines help students memorize the movements that make up the system. These include both bare-hand and weapons routines. The routines are more than just part of the curriculum: they actually preserve the core of the martial systems.

Many become fanatical about perfecting the routines. Over years, many repetitions certainly train a student for better body mechanics, and improve balance and power. At the same time, regular practice maintains health. Students seeking specific routines enjoy learning the applications and feeling strong, and perhaps they delight in showing others the high-level skills they have attained. Practicing routines is a wonderful way to embody the above goals, which are substantial in themselves. But there is a clear line that distinguishes a solo routine from a practical fighting art.

Martial arts need not necessarily be studied as martial, but a true martial art must be realistic in combat and self-defense. Practicing routines may help students reach this objective, but there are more stages to include in the learning curriculum to be useful for fighting. Solo routines do not bring in aspects of the reality of facing an opponent. Between the defender and attacker comes the matter of timing. A perfectly executed technique is meaningless if not done at the right time. An excellent technique started too close or too far away from the opponent fails. The distance is not appropriate. The defender must know how and when to move to execute techniques against an opponent who is also moving. Shooting an arrow at a stationary target is much easier than shooting at one in motion. Plus, the targets may unpredictably change directions.

Practicing the set patterns in routines does not fully prepare one for the spontaneity necessary to perform applications in any violent confrontations. Martial arts taught for realistic situations include additional forms of practice, such as practicing applications in pairs. Two-person application practice starts slow, but over weeks and months the speed is increased. As students' skills increase, they begin to practice against multiple attackers. Training includes weaponry. All such training hones one's skills to be effective in realistic situations. At this level, the martial artist performs with power, speed, and accuracy, with the ability to improvise spontaneously.

Teacher-Disciple Relationship

In Chinese culture, the relationship between parents and their children is the most important relationship a child will ever experience. Perhaps this outlook stems from Confucianism, or just from natural inclination—maybe both. For better or worse, the parents' influence is highly significant in every way. One's life is a gift from the parents, a life nurtured for years from birth to adulthood. As parents age, the role is reversed, and the child cares for the parents.

In traditional martial arts, styles are unique and preserved through a teacher-disciple relationship, making this of supreme importance for the lineage. Like familial heritage, a martial art style is valued for what is inherited and passed to the next generation. While not necessarily a blood relation, to become a formal disciple is to join a martial family, and the relationships are as follows:

Shifu: This form of address is often translated into Western languages as "master," but it is more than that. The compound is made of two characters, *shi* meaning "tutor" and *fu* meaning "father." The shifu, the grandmaster of a system, could be either male or female. The title is even more significant than *laoshi*, translated as "teacher" and referring to a teacher who is an elder and hence has experience and knowledge. Other common terms of important martial family relationships include the following:

Shimu: master-mother (shifu's wife)
Shibo: senior uncle
Shishu: junior uncle
Shizhang: master-husband (female master's husband)
Tudi: apprentice/disciple
Dashixiong: biggest brother
Shixiong: big brother
Shidi: little brother
Shijie: big sister
Shimei: little sister

A master could have many students, but only a small number would be "adopted" into the system and entrusted to carry on the lineage. The master handpicks these disciples, who participate in an elaborate ceremony called *baishi*, or "respecting the master," to formalize the status. During the ceremony they pledge allegiance to the shifu, including a pledge not to study with any other teacher unless given permission. Like a real son or daughter, they respect the shifu as they do a parent, and they honor the reputation of the school. They pledge to cultivate their own character as well as the art, and to protect the tradition and teachings.

As a sign of appreciation, the disciple expresses reverence by kneeling in front of the shifu, bowing fully three times, each time with the forehead touching the ground (*ketou*). Afterward, the disciple may sip tea with the teacher and give him gifts, including a red envelope with money inside, a common gesture demonstrating that disciples value their shifu and his or her teachings. Rather than by age, disciples are listed by seniority according to when they are officially adopted. After the ceremony, they are referred to as "indoor" disciples, and they receive all the teachings of the school. Along with this honor comes not only knowledge, but the tremendous responsibility of the future of the school and its teachings.

Manchu Military

Chongzhen [1611–1644], the last emperor of the Ming Dynasty, failed to quell peasant rebellions and the advance of the Manchu army. In great despair, he hanged himself north of the Forbidden City, in Jingshan Park, not far from where I stand now. The Manchus founded the Qing Dynasty by military conquest and, over a hundred years later, they still maintain rule in glorious fashion with strong armed forces, primarily based on horsemanship and archery. Thus, the Mandate of Heaven is evident in the prosperity of today, under a minority of two million Manchus ruling one hundred million Han Chinese.

As an aficionado of the martial arts, I find the evolution of combat interesting, from the village level up to the scale of great nations. Even the character for country, *guo*, shows a border as protected by weapons. We have two standing armies. The Manchu Banner army is over two hundred thousand strong. Half are garrisoned in Beijing, and the other half guard major cities. The second army of predominantly Han Chinese is the Green Standard troops. Twice the size of the Banner Army, the Green Standard troops are garrisoned throughout the country.

Between 1775 and 1779, Qing troops stabilized the northern and western boundaries of Xinjiang Province, harshly squelching the rebellion in the area occupied by the Mongolic Zunghar tribe. We have new paintings illustrating some of the famous battles that took place. More than five hundred thousand were eliminated, with only fifty Mongols fleeing for their lives. Mongol influence was curtailed, Tibet came under our control, and we brought in other minorities to repopulate the area, such as the Islamic Hui and Uyghurs. In western Sichuan Province, the Jinchuan hill people were also suppressed [1747–1749]. However, the recent invasions into Burma [1765–1769] proved disastrous for Qianlong's armies, with over seventy thousand soldiers and four commanders dying. I'm sure the emperor will soon send another force. Since the British arrival of merchant ships in the seventeenth century, Emperor Qianlong wisely decided in 1757 to confine all foreign trade to Guangzhou city. Because of all such measures, the security of our heartland could enjoy peace and the bounties of life.

Many weapons were needed for military expeditions, so Emperor Qianlong realized a need to standardize the design and making of offensive and defensive weapons. The new products included longbows, helmets, lances, swords, long-bladed sabers, spears, and muskets. Based on a 1759 document, the *Huangchao Liqi Tushi* offers a list of weapons with details as to their making. Along with the many long and short weapons, we can add matchlock guns, since we've used them ever since the Portuguese introduced them during the Ming Dynasty. Under the Kangxi Emperor (1662–1722), firearms were certainly a very important part of the military. Dai Zi recently invented the continuous-shot gun, which delivers twenty-eight bullets in succession. This is an improvement upon the "swarm of bees," a thirty-two–shot multiple rocket-arrow launcher from the Ming Dynasty. The Qing Dynasty's success is due to its fine balance of attention to both civil and military matters. We see martial values constantly present in our culture, including in literature, art, and architecture.

Since I am originally from a small town in Henan, I still favor the martial practices associated with individuals rather than those of mass military operations. The regional governors do maintain local militias for the province, and this includes even small villages. In our daily observations, we come in contact with martial arts relating to the country, province, and village. In contrast to the life of a professional soldier, there is more to enjoy in martial practice as an individual with a small circle of like-minded friends.

Battle Scene of the Quelling of Rebellions in the Western Regions, detail. Etching print (1759) by Giuseppe Castiglione. *Cleveland Museum of Art. Public domain.*

Laws of Boxing

Ever since the Jesuit Matteo Ricci and Xu Guangqi published a translation of the first six books of Euclid's *Elements* into Chinese in 1614, Western mathematical concepts have given us a new way to look at the world. Often while practicing martial arts in my courtyard, I think of the geometry of movement and the very structure of the human body. How do we move? What are the relationships between body parts? Can I improve my fighting skills using mathematical laws and applications?

Every combat posture has a shape, and every technique is made by a series of movements, flowing from posture to posture. For the martial arts, I usually first look at the individual postures as static architectural designs. There is a foundation upon which the other parts rest, under the influences of weight and gravity. Such a special balance of the human form! It always amazes me how many combat postures can be made and meet all the criteria of structural integrity. It's not unlike how thousands of Chinese characters can be individually written within a square, and each character will retain balance among all the parts.

Martial arts are not stagnant, so the physics of movement come into play in the quest to understand them. We see living geometry in movement—the straight punch, an angled push, a circling kick, openings and closings, compression and expansion, and more. So, I spend much time in studying each movement. Proper alignment is crucial to optimize each movement while limiting any possible damage to the body. This certainly gives strength to positions and power to movements.

Our understanding of static postures versus moving techniques affects how we practice martial arts and their effectiveness in application. Many practitioners try to use the laws of static postures in their actions. As the properties of ice and liquid water are different, so are the properties for martial arts. Being still and balanced is not the same as balanced movement. The sources of power for a straight strike are different from those of a curved strike.

We perform martial arts in time and space according to our bodily condition. Our practice involves awareness of how we actually move, utilizing our muscle power, flexibility, breathing, skeletal range of motion, and more. As we learn more about the kinetics of our own body movement, we can better understand how and why martial arts are utilized against any adversary—whose movements are also governed by those same laws of physics.

Less than ten miles from the center of Beijing is the Lugou Bridge, or what some call the Marco Polo Bridge. It was originally built more than five hundred years ago over the Yongding River. Following flood damage, it was reconstructed by orders of the Kangxi Emperor in 1698. Built fifty years prior at the eastern end of the bridge is the Wanping Fortress. Both the stone bridge and the fortress show the architects' understanding of how structures are built for strength and to withstand assault by military force as well as natural elements. This gives us an opportunity to see how the stonework of bridges and fortifications relates to our martial arts.

A fortress is built mainly for defense. The walls must be high and thick, with the ability to withstand bombardment by cannons. A bridge is designed to span the width of a river and support heavy weight by any transport over it. However, if the pressures on the bridge are more than what is physically possible for the structure to support, it will collapse. The common principle derived from this example is applied for self-defense, making stable postures that cannot be unsettled by an opponent. As a result, many practitioners strengthen their bodies through an assortment of exercises. They also experiment to find the most formidable postures for attacking and defending.

Martial artists must fortify their bodies: the many masters I've met over the past decades agree with this—all except one. He believed one should strive for perfect body alignment for techniques, but then not rely on it for strength. His theory proved exceptional by testing. He could throw opponents easily in all directions, while others only searched to find his center. It was like trying to grasp smoke. He was skilled enough to manage any attack without tension. Here are a few examples he used to illustrate the principles.

Let's consider two people of equal strength. The attacker throws a right punch. The defender steps to the left side to avoid the oncoming punch. He simultaneously circles his arms out left to right, deflecting the oncoming arm at the wrist with his right forearm and the elbow with his left hand. Without stopping, he continues the movement to bring the opponent's arm against him while stepping in with a simultaneous push.

If the opponent resists and the push is made directly forward with arms parallel to the ground, the push will most likely fail. Even if the one pushing is stronger, the physics are not favorable. The person resisting can supplement his resisting force from the strength of his rear leg against the ground. In reality, this makes the one trying to push feel he is trying to move the earth. He's pushing into the opponent's arms toward his core, leg, and earth. Rather than pushing parallel with the ground, it becomes much easier to change the trajectory of the push slightly upward, which cuts the other's connection between his back leg and ground. Often, if one throws a punch that is blocked or deflected, he will retreat. This makes the push even easier if the momentum is timed with the retreat.

Perhaps another example will make it easier to see the valuable use of angles in offense and defense. Have someone face you in a right forward stance with his right arm in a defensive position, palm facing his chest. Get into a right stance, placing your right hand near his wrist and the other toward his elbow. Slowly push as he resists, and gradually add more strength. Both sides will increase proportionally with force against force being equal. A great amount of tension can be reached. The foot placement is excellent to resist or push frontward.

Now, rather than push forward, take your right hand, place it on the opponent's left shoulder, and push him from right to left, which is roughly 90 degrees from the line made with his feet. It should be an easily successful push. You can also take one step to the right side and then push in the same direction. Although his feet are in a strong position for resisting from the front, they will not help him resist from the side.

We see that some angles are more favorable for attacking than other angles. Likewise, some angles are more easily defended. Every stance has strong and weak points. It is to our benefit to learn the value of angles for defense and offense.

Analysis and Intuition

Some of my summers were spent up north at the Chengde Mountain Resort, where the emperors go to escape sweltering Beijing. In order to carry on all the regular activities usually done at the capital, the expansive area there includes palaces, administrative offices, and ceremonial buildings. I often had the opportunity to attend concerts of Shaoyue—royal court music. The musical instruments included ancient bronze bells, jade chime stones, bamboo flutes, drums, and stringed instruments. The melodies and resonance are so rapturous!

As I recollect the playing by those professional musicians at the summer resort, I realize there is a parallel in their art and the martial arts. We had the opportunity to hear the musicians in their prime, playing to perfection and energized by emotions. However, these musicians were not born with this talent. They went through a learning process. I discussed this with some of the famous musicians, and they explained how they mastered their instruments.

Royal court music is extremely complex, based on a five-tone scale and varied time signatures, syncopations, and rhythmic changes. In brief, it takes much time to learn how to read music scores. On top of this is learning how to play an instrument itself. The goal of becoming a master of court music is daunting. The learning process is one devoted to study, memorizing, analyzing, correcting, and years of practice.

In this chosen music field, a number of players reach a point where they can read and play from a score. Their sound may seem somewhat lifeless, as they must concentrate so much on the mechanics. However, a few break through the mental restraints by becoming so skilled that they reach a transitional point where they don't need to rely on reading sheet music or think of where notes are located on their instruments. They attain an ability to play with less thinking and more feeling. The music comes alive.

The martial artist goes through the same learning process as the musician. We also must be devoted to study, memorizing, analyzing, correcting, and years of practice. Few are so resolute to reach a master level in the art, and even fewer can transition to the more intuitive level of playing. A sharp intellect is required to analyze and remember all the techniques, but often—when the mind remains occupied by thought—it is too difficult to let emotions and intuition enter one's performance.

Some musicians and martial artists are too cerebral to allow a pure flow in their techniques. A musician who stutters while playing loses the intended melody. A martial artist who stutters in movement loses his life! Thinking disrupts playing and movement. Through years of practice it becomes possible to transition to a more intuitive level. At this level, one's skills are so embodied that techniques emerge according to the situation. The Dao of the music and the Dao of the martial are one.

Pleasing the Eyes

All the arts in China display a great variety of skills and styles, as would be expected. We have many ethnic groups making their imprint, growing Western influences, and a strong impact from the Manchus. From the amateur to the most skilled, art flourishes throughout China today. This includes the martial arts. As a discipline that focuses on body movement, the fighting arts have much in common with other physical activities, such as dance, sports, and many endeavors of daily life that require specialized skills. Even animals delight us by the ways they can move—a monkey's acrobatics in the trees, a galloping horse, a hawk's maneuvers, a frog's leap, or a carp's glide through waters.

In the martial arts we instantly recognize many of the qualities we associate with the beauty of movement. We often judge performances by the standards we feel appropriate. These can include grace, fluidity, strength, balance, accuracy, tempo, coordination, control, flexibility, and other qualities. Even though we see so much beauty in the martial arts, they are not so easy to judge. Some are extravagant to the point of being outlandish. Others are so subtle that most people don't notice their hidden secrets.

All styles work with the inborn qualities of the human body and the natural environment. For example, regardless of style, any jump is done with considerations of gravity. Martial artists become acutely aware of the body's capabilities, variations in muscular tensions, the expenditure of energy, and moving through time and space. In addition to the physical, martial art performance brings joy from movement, especially when done in inspiring environments. The state of mind of the performer is intimately connected to the activity.

Martial arts can challenge the most gifted practitioner to reach for perfection of human movement. When practiced wisely, they instruct one into the uniqueness of body-mind movement. Our medical and scientific experts can provide details on the many possible health benefits derived from this. All these aspects play their part in describing the beauty inherent in the martial arts. The joy of creating such wondrous beauty is prime motivation to practice them.

Wave Currents

If you've walked on roads in Xingjiang Province, you may have been nearly pushed over by a strong gust of wind. Or, if you've stood on the beach in Qingdao, Shandong Province, you may have watched strong tides of the Yellow Sea crashing onto the shoreline. The wave patterns of wind and air are replicated in many combat techniques. By themselves, air and water are neutral. The resulting damage they can cause does not directly come from them, but from the source of power that moves them. The fist does not throw itself but is powered outward, like a cannonball toward a target.

Another example of wave movement is seen in the actions of a whip. One holds the wooden handle and swings it backward then forward, directing the leather strip toward a target. The leather is neutral, but it is the person who directs it outward to snap with great impact. With wind, water, or leather, we can notice a rolling movement toward a specific point. A wave of energy moves outward like a current from the source of power.

Those new to martial arts usually try to push solely with arm power or kick solely with leg power. Of course these methods work, but they reflect a low skill level. High-level masters use a wavelike whole-body movement, which is more efficient and produces greater power. We can look at a forward two-hand push as an illustration.

Start by standing in a forward stance with both arms facing the front. Think of moving the hips in a circle: start to shift back and downward, sinking on the back leg, and then shift forward, following a curved path. The backward movement also draws the arms in toward the chest. Lower your body with the sinking motion, and then project the hands to curve upward to the front.

Practice the above with an attacker moving toward you with a two-hand push. By your circling movement, your forearms move upward to meet his incoming attack, drawing him toward you but deflecting his arms outward. As he tries to retreat, continue circling your hips downward, then upward to execute your push.

Important here is to let the hands follow your body. When you move back, you may at first be moving away from your hands! As the body reaches its maximum backward movement, your arms will catch up to the chest. Then, as you start to shift forward, the hands start to push. As the body reaches its maximum forward movement, the arms continue forward. Throughout this entire movement, energy comes from the legs and is directed by the waist. The end of the movement, the push, results from whole-body motion. As a wave, the energy travels from the legs through the body's core, to the arms and then the hands. It is a tremendous current of power. If the hands are on an opponent, that person receives the force. This type of wave force only works if the body is relaxed while moving quickly. Any stiffness will hamper the movement. Water and air do not have tensions, yet they can emit great force.

Experiment with the concept of wave currents in various techniques. Hand techniques are the easiest to visualize and implement. Leg techniques utilize this principle too, but it may take time to figure out how this is possible. For example, a kick shouldn't start by moving the leg first. It usually starts by shifting and turning the waist. The waist movement draws the thigh into position, and the rest of the leg follows. A wave still flows through the body to the foot. Even a shoulder strike can utilize a wave current, as in shifting, turning the waist, and propelling the shoulder in succession.

Using the wave current correctly creates a beautiful technique. When attempted with any tensions, the results can be quite comical. It will take some years of practice to perform techniques properly. Don't give up. The patience and time invested are worth it.

Meditation: Training the Mind

About three thousand years ago, Zhuangzi wrote about *zuowang*: sitting and forgetting. Since then a very rich array of meditating techniques has developed. There are influences from India, but most now are associated with Buddhism and Daoism, which share many common features. Meditative practices have influenced martial traditions for good reason.

Buddhist meditation is strongly spiritual, with a quest for enlightenment, a transcendent state of consciousness. Daoist meditation is also for clearing the mind but with a focus on health and longevity. The foundation of these two traditions rests on methods to calm the mind. The standard physical practice is to sit in a stationary position, but some schools stand, lie down, or include rhythmic movements. Regardless of the physical posture, the mental exercises are of primary importance.

A common meditative practice is to focus the mind on one thing, such as the breath or a candle flame. Some schools favor visualizing organs of the body, specific deities, or the energetic pathways. Others think about mental travels to a sacred mountain peak, a foreign country, or even to the moon. The diversity of meditative methods brings noted benefits, including a release of tensions and mental clarity.

What specifically does meditation have to offer the martial artist? To answer this question, we need to look at how one performs in combat. When one is in any serious violent confrontation, it is usual to become overwhelmed by fear. Tensions run through the body, breathing becomes difficult, and confusion enters the mind. These can cripple even a good martial artist. Meditative practices relieve tensions and train one to maintain a calm mind; thus, they are helpful to prepare martial artists to function during combat. A tranquil mind also steadies emotions that might otherwise cloud one's judgment and adversely affect fighting skills.

An additional benefit is that meditation fosters an increase in awareness of self and surroundings. When one is more self-aware, combat techniques are easier to master. While fighting, it is advantageous to be mindful of opponents and the environment.

Telling a student to relax helps very little. Relax the face, neck, shoulders, wrists . . . and any physical resulting change will prove temporary. The tensions quickly return. But why? Tensions may permeate the body, but the solution is not physical. In most cases, tensions come from the state of mind. Fear and anger are big factors. So, meditative techniques prove helpful to the martial artist. Training is more productive. Skills improve. Health is nurtured.

Martial Ingenuity

Even before the early Xia Dynasty [c. 2070 to c. 1600 BCE], when the great tribal ancestors were prospering in the Yellow River Valley, weapons were used against animals and humans. The spear, which offered a measure of safety by providing distance, was the primary tool for hunting as well as warfare. What a tremendous development in warfare since that early period!

Many people are not aware of just how much the fighting arts have evolved and what they have offered to our civilization. From the technical perspective, we know these arts are used for offense, including strikes, throws, locks, and breaks. This is a simplified description. The functions can be multiplied a thousandfold.

Strikes? What kind of strike? A hand strike can be made with one or more knuckles, backhand, edges, or palm. Locks may be of single or multiple joint areas. Some masters can actually lock the whole body, totally immobilizing a subject smoothly and quickly! In our lives we rarely get to see the full range of possible combat techniques. Masters with the greatest skills wisely guard their knowledge from the public. What we do see is a relatively narrow glimpse. Add the enormous variety of weapons, and the depth of knowledge is truly difficult to comprehend.

Fighting techniques are not just movements. We must remember they were devised with detailed knowledge of anatomy and psychology. At high levels of practice, masters know how to attack the external and internal parts of the body, including the vital points as discussed in medical treaties. Offensive attacks can also be directed psychologically, causing fear and loss of confidence to those attacked. The tools here can be very subtle, such as in dress, design of weapon, speech, and deportment.

Adding to the body of knowledge of offensive combat is the equally enormous body of knowledge for defense. Much here is interrelated, but the knowledge and techniques may be applied differently, as in evading attacks, escaping from holds, and countering actions.

If the depth and breadth of Chinese martial arts were to be presented in writing, a multivolume encyclopedia would result. It would include an overview of all the individual fighting techniques, practice routines, and partner drills for bare hand and weapons. Medical information would accompany aspects of health and longevity. The studies of human anatomy would show what occurs in the body while in movement or results of receiving techniques. When we see all such details, we experience a greater appreciation for the martial traditions. We understand how martial art practice can draw out the great potential of the human body and mind.

Martial Arts, Religion, and Healing

Martial artists are integral to every level of society: village, provincial, and national. They represent individual clan styles, regional systems, and combatives associated with the mighty Qing forces. Regardless of their social position, they share a common ground in the fighting arts and the associated life-threatening hazards. The possibility of death or injury is ever present in their lives, so it is natural for martial artists to hold high regard for religion, health, and medical treatment.

A martial artist cannot help but think of mortality. What comes after death? Have you made preparations to leave this world? The primary source for answers comes from spiritual traditions. Buddhism, beginning with a warrior prince named Siddhartha Gautama, is associated with the premise that life is suffering. The path to escape suffering is detachment. This idea fits well for one who must face combat. It frees the mind and the emotions that cloud it, preparing a fighter to be totally present. Buddhist meditative practices are useful for attaining this mental state. The doctrine of reincarnation gives a fighter a vision of transmigration to another life stage, or perhaps enlightenment. Fighting for a good cause also builds good karma, the actions that move one on to a better place.

Daoist meditative practices help one to prepare the mind for battle, much the same as the Buddhist tradition. There are related practices that help one physically prepare for combat, such as specialized stretching, breathing exercises, and cultivating inner energy. Many accept Daoist tales of immortals living in the Kunlun Mountains and on five islands off the coast of Shandong Province in the Bohai Sea. Daoists are known for performing superhuman feats. They have convinced many that they too can be invincible and become immortal.

Because martial artists can get injured, there is need for medical and healing skills and techniques. Many masters include this as part of their teaching. They can heal bruises, fractures, cuts, and other injuries that may occur through practice or actual combat. Some of the training is preventive, but much is restorative. The modalities include acupuncture, moxibustion, bone setting, massage, and herbal treatments. In extreme cases, we must call on specialists, such as surgeons.

The Yellow Emperor's Medicine Classic has been a standard reference for nearly two thousand years. Today we also have the great encyclopedia, the *Collection of Ancient and Modern Works*, published in 1726. It includes about 520 chapters on medicine. Even newer is the *Golden Mirror of Medicine*, by Wu Qian in 1742.

Serious martial artists are interested in continuously developing their skills and deepening their knowledge. Combatives have a natural affiliation with religious, health, and healing traditions. Advanced masters believe that if you can cause harm, you should also be able to heal—a balancing of yin and yang.

I had many questions about boxing styles for Liu Pingsan, my teacher on Wudang Mountain.

"Which is the most practical of the Wudang styles? Are there any outstanding qualities found in the Shaolin, Muslim, Southern, and other Northern styles?"

"No," he said. "They all have strengths and weaknesses, especially when we consider who presents the style. An excellent style illustrated by a person without much talent will not look very promising. A poor style done by one with superior talent will certainly appear formidable."

Master Liu advised against deciding which style or technique is good by reputation alone.

"Don't rely on place of origin, style name, or the words of a famous master," he said. "And, don't believe in anything I say because you trust me. Teachers' beliefs and actions are not above question, but the masters should always be respected for their good intentions and concern for their students."

I felt in the dark on how to proceed with my martial art studies, but Master Liu offered some good suggestions.

"Observe the various styles and techniques regardless of their origin and reputation," he said. "Listen to any teacher you are fortunate to meet."

Then, seemingly sidetracked, he started to discuss the rich herbal traditions and how the herbal pharmacopeia expanded over the centuries. Since Shennong, the "Divine Farmer," wrote his *Materia Medica* over two thousand years ago, many more lifesaving remedies have been added. Some came from mountain hermits, others from government-sponsored medical schools. The herbs used come from every corner of the country, and even outside our borders. Master Liu tied this history to the martial arts.

"Thousands of herbs have been tested to learn of their unique healing powers," he said. "Even poisons can be used as cures! Good idea to test carefully!"

He said the exact same process helps the martial arts evolve.

"Gather information and techniques whenever possible, from whoever you can. As in your case, your teacher gave you permission to study with other teachers. Your level is already high, so he introduced you to other masters. Also learn from observing those involved in other human activities that can indirectly relate, such as construction workers, cooks, and farmers. Learn from nature. See how a bamboo bends, water flows, and lightening strikes."

In the end, Master Liu's advice was that the efficiency of any martial technique needs to be tested in as realistic a way as possible and proven. He stressed that we should examine theories that look promising, as well as theories that may seem obviously faulty. We may be surprised at what we can learn!

Afterword

It wasn't his intention, but Yang Mingbin provided us with a special view of Chinese martial arts in the mid-eighteenth century. The notes he made were for himself and perhaps for his Jesuit friend, Giuseppe Castiglione. His writings didn't focus on one particular style, its history, or techniques. He was looking deeper. The sixty-four topics deal with practical martial principles and the joyous process of learning.

Yang was a man of his times, but not the common sort. Living during the Qing Dynasty, at its height of cultural splendor, he was witness to a rare unfolding of history in one of the world's greatest capital cities. As the Northern Manchus were conquering China, they adopted the Chinese culture, including ways of governing and even clothing styles. Rather than subjugate the conquered with totally servile status, they placed Chinese in many official positions. Some Chinese welcomed them as true inheritors of the Mandate of Heaven, with the succession of Manchu kings becoming the Sons of Heaven and legitimate rulers by natural order from 1644 to 1912.

Being from a small village in Henan, Yang must have had exceptional artistic skills to become a painter at the royal court. He was well educated and well traveled. In Beijing he worked in an international atmosphere of openness and cooperation. He was surrounded by artistic splendors of every medium, ancient and modern. This included arts and sciences from the West.

What we have learned of Yang's life in Beijing sheds light on how he came to be a martial arts master. He had an eye for detail. Painters must be keen observers, and he had this gift for studying combatives as well. While many were xenophobic, Yang was very open to other people and cultures. He loved philosophy, Eastern and Western. He developed a way of learning that benefited him in every field: painting, martial arts, music, culture, and probably many more areas.

We don't have all the details about Yang's martial arts background, but we know he studied in a traditional way under his first master. He enjoyed a fine reputation among other martial artists, and many accepted him within their circles. They would only do so if they trusted him and admired his character.

Master Yang was a pioneer. His way of thinking was encompassing. He viewed the martial arts as one and whole—and individual styles as but branches. We hope that by presenting his notes in this book, many today will benefit from Yang Mingbin's place in martial art history. May he inspire further research, practice, and development of this cherished and multifaceted discipline of Chinese martial culture.

Left: The character Dao from the brush of Master Yang Qingyu. Below: Chinese double-edge straight sword. The Metropolitan Museum of Art, New York. Bequest of George C. Stone, 1935. Public domain. Accession Number: 36.25.1484a

In 1976, DeMarco began studies with Master Yang in this area of 228 Peace Memorial Park, Taipei. Photos taken 2017.

Master Yang Qingyu and Michael DeMarco in Puli, Taiwan, 1989.

Master Yang in Puli, Taiwan, 1989.

Chinese characters for

Yang
Mingbin

Glossary

Baduanjin	Eight Pieces of Brocade	八段錦
baishi	apprenticeship ceremony	拜師
Da Qing Lü Li	Great Qing Law	大清律例
Dao	way, road, path	道﹝首﹞﹝辶﹞
Baiyun Guan	White Cloud Monastery	白雲觀
dashixiong	biggest brother	大師兄
ershijie	second biggest sister	二師姐
fa	law	法﹝氵﹞﹝去﹞
guo	country	國
Huang Jingjie	(translator of this book)	黃靜傑
ketou	tap head (to prostrate, to bow)	磕頭
Lang Shining	Giuseppe Castiglione	郎世寧
li	texture, order	理
linggan	inspiration	靈感
Liuzijue	Six Healing Sounds	六字訣
neidan	internal alchemy	內丹
sanshimei	third biggest sister	三師妹
shibo	senior uncle	師伯
shidi	little brother	師弟
shifu	teacher-father	師父
shijie	big sister	師姐
shimei	little sister	師妹
shimu	master's mother	師母
shishu	junior uncle	師叔
shixiong	big brother	師兄
shizhang	master-husband	師丈
tudi	apprentice, disciple	徒弟
waidan	external alchemy	外丹
Xuqinxi	Five Animal Frolics	五禽戲
yali	pressure	壓力
Yang Mingbin	(author of this book)	楊明璸
Yang Qingyu	(author's ancestor in Taiwan)	楊清玉
Yang Yingyin	(author's ancestor in Henan)	楊映銀
Yijinjing	*Muscle-Tendon Classic*	易筋經
zuowang	sitting and forgetting	坐忘

Index